The Amish Widow

Amish Secret Widows Society Book 1

Samantha Price

Copyright © 2015 by Samantha Price

All rights reserved.

No part of this book may be reproduced in any form or by any electronic or mechanical means, including information storage and retrieval systems, without written permission from the author, except for the use of brief quotations in a book review.

Scripture quotations from The Authorized (King James) Version. Rights in the Authorized Version in the United Kingdom are vested in the Crown. Reproduced by permission of the Crown's patentee, Cambridge University Press.

This is a work of fiction. Any names or characters, businesses or places, events or incidents, are fictitious. Any resemblance to actual persons, living or dead, or actual events is purely coincidental.

Chapter One

*To every thing there is a season, and a time to
every purpose under the heaven:
A time to be born, and a time to die; a time to plant,
and a time to pluck up that which is planted;*
Ecclesiastes 3:1-2

"Why did you leave me?"

Emma Kurtzler stared at the body of her late husband. Of course, she didn't expect him to respond, but she felt as if she deserved some kind of answer. Why did he have to die when everything in her life was just the way she had always dreamed it would be?

The rumbling of muffled conversations from the crowd in the next room made Emma aware that her time with Levi was drawing to a close. As was custom in Emma's Amish community, the body laid in the *familye haus* before being taken to the cemetery.

Emma smoothed Levi's hair back with two fingers and touched his hands, which were placed across his chest. "Oh, Levi, you don't even look like you anymore." It was true, the body that lay before her was Levi, but there was a different feeling about him, as if he were someone else. In a way, she wanted to keep him there, right in the house with her forever, but she couldn't – that would be weird.

The noises from the other room distracted her once more. Levi would soon have to go to the cemetery, his body's final resting place. She touched her stomach lightly, knowing there was a chance that there might be a little *boppli* inside. If there were, then she would have a piece of Levi with her forever; she would have someone to love and wouldn't be alone.

"Emma, are you ready for everyone to come in now?"

Emma looked up to see the solidly built, dark-haired Wil, who had been Levi's best friend and constant companion. Levi and Wil were complete opposites, which was most likely the very thing that had drawn them together. Levi had been stable and dependable, whereas Wil was flighty, full of fancy notions and always thinking of grand ideas for new gadgets. Sometimes Emma found Wil funny, at other times tiresome, but on this day she didn't know what she would have done without him.

"Just one more minute, Wil. Just one more minute."

Wil bowed his head and left the room. Emma heard him say something to the crowd in the living room and a hush fell.

"I have to go now. I guess *Gott* wanted you home for some reason." A tear trickled down her cheek and dropped onto the black fabric of Levi's suit. She had made sure that he was dressed in the same suit that he had worn on their wedding day.

With the back of her hand, she wiped the damp from her cheek. "I guess I won't be far behind you. We all have to go sometime, don't we?" At that moment, Emma wished that she had been the one to die. If *Gott* wanted one of them home, couldn't it have been her? Why did He have to take Levi?

Emma put her fingers to her lips and then placed them on Levi's forehead before turning and opening the door for the waiting group of relatives and friends. Some folk smiled at Emma as they filed past to see Levi, while others offered their condolences. After a few minutes in the crowded room her head began to swim.

"You okay, Emma?"

Emma knew it was Wil beside her. "I need some air."

He ushered her through the crowd and out into the open for some fresh air. Once outside, Emma felt much better. She took a little walk along the row of buggies and drew in a deep breath. As she exhaled, she caught sight of her reflection in the window of a buggy. At first, she hardly recognized herself; she seemed much smaller and thinner, her cheeks sunken from too much crying. She studied her reflection and adjusted her white starched prayer *kapp*, reminding herself to put on her black over-bonnet before she headed to the cemetery.

Emma swung around to talk to Wil, who was still standing close by. "*Denke*, Wil, for helping me these last few days. I really don't know what I would've done without you, with my parents not being able to make it here and everything."

"Emma, you don't have to thank me. Levi and I were like *bruders*, so I guess that makes you like my *schweschder*." He laughed as he tried to make light of the situation. When Emma remained silent, with no hint of a smile on her face, he added, "I'd do anything for you, Emma, remember that. If you need anything, please ask me, whatever it is."

"Okay, *denke*."

"I mean it, Emma. Look at me."

Emma looked into his deep brown eyes and noticed for the first time how beautiful they were. Not that she would ever – or could ever – be interested in another *mann;* certainly not the very flighty and unstable Wil. She continued to look at him, but he didn't speak. *"Jah,* Wil?"

"I want you to know you can rely on me for anything. House repairs, buggy repairs, anything at all – I'll be there."

Emma dragged her eyes away from him. *"Denke.* I will remember that." It warmed her heart that she lived within such a close-knit community of caring people and wouldn't have to be alone.

Wil looked over her shoulder. "Don't look now, but Elsa-May and Ettie are headed this way."

Elsa-May and Ettie were two elderly sisters, both widows. Up until a few days ago, Emma had not had anything in common with the funny old ladies. Now, she knew the heartache they must have gone through when they lost their husbands. The bonds of loss united them.

"There you are, dear. How are you feeling?" Ettie was the more gentle, soft-spoken of the two, whereas her *schweschder,* Elsa-May, was loud and to the point.

Before Emma had a chance to open her mouth, Elsa-May said, "Oh, Ettie, how do you think she'd be feeling?"

Ettie wrung her hands. "Oh dear – I'm sorry, Emma. I'm always saying the wrong thing."

Emma smiled at Ettie and put a comforting hand on her shoulder. *"Nee.* That's fine. I appreciate your kindness." Emma guessed the two of them to be in their seventies, or perhaps even their eighties.

There were two other widows in the community, Silvie and Maureen, who were much younger. Even though she wasn't close to many people, Maureen was Emma's dearest friend. She was the kind of person that people liked instantly from the moment they saw her. Maureen was a large woman with a most generous smile, one couldn't help but smile back at her. Her face was round and glowed with an inner radiance, and she had a delightful small gap between her two front teeth. Maureen had been a widow for some time, but her husband had been unwell for many years so his death had not been unexpected.

Like Maureen and Silvie, Emma was childless unless *Gott* showed His kindness – she wouldn't be sure for another couple of weeks.

Emma couldn't even count all the buggies that made up the procession to the cemetery.

Standing by the graveside, Emma looked around her. Everyone was dressed in black. Never in her wildest dreams did she think she would have been widowed so young. She and Levi had barely started their lives together.

The bishop walked forward and cleared his throat. Emma had respectfully asked him to be brief in what he said at the graveside. She didn't think she could take a long, drawn-out sermon and the bishop was extremely fond of long, drawn-out sermons. He had agreed to keep it short.

He preached the usual funeral jargon that Emma had heard so many times before. We all return to the dust of the ground – not very cheerful. Neither was life being likened to a vapor that is here one minute and gone the next. Emma closed her eyes and replaced the bishop's words with Levi's smiling face, happy to be home with the Lord at last; that made Emma feel better. She mentally blocked out the words about the 'dust of the fields' and the 'vapor.'

It was after Levi had been placed in the ground and everyone was returning to their buggies that Wil whispered to Emma, "Who is that *Englischer* standing over there? Do you know him?"

She followed Wil's gaze. Emma had not even noticed the *Englischer*. She stared at the stranger and he stared back before walking toward her. "I don't know him at all, but he's coming this way."

"Looks like you'll soon find out," Wil said.

"Good morning, Mrs. Kurtzler."

Emma nodded hello to the stout man with thinning gray hair. By the look of his suit and the shine on his fine leather shoes, Emma presumed him to be quite wealthy.

"It's likely not a good time, but I'm here to make you an offer for your land," the stranger said.

Wil put his strong arm between the two of them and turned Emma away from the man. "She'll not talk of business today, or of anything like that. Good day to you." Wil steered Emma away.

She glanced over her shoulder at the man to see

that he was still looking at her with desperation written all over his face. Emma had just inherited Levi's prime parcel of farming land. Levi had leased it out to Henry Pluver, an Amish man who also leased other Amish farms, including Wil's.

Once they were a distance away, Wil moved his arm from Emma's back.

"I wonder why he wants the land," Emma mused as she looked around for the Pluver family. Surely they would be at the funeral. She caught sight of the three of them standing together – Mr. and Mrs. Pluver and their only son, Bob. The Pluver family kept to themselves, but Mrs. Pluver seemed a most unhappy woman and their son never spoke to anyone. Bob worked with his father and, as far as Emma knew, he had no friends.

Wil shook his head. "Vultures, nothing but vultures. I'm sorry, Emma. I should have gone over and asked him what he was doing here or who he was."

"You weren't to know. It's not unusual to have *Englischers* at one of our funerals. Levi's boss and the men he worked with are all here; for all you knew, he could've been one of them." Levi had worked for one of the new high-rise building construction companies. Emma had been told that Levi had refused the mandatory safety harness, and a sudden downpour of rain caused him to slip on his footings. Emma was shocked when she'd learned that he had refused the safety harness, as Levi was normally such a stickler for rules.

Wil whispered to Emma, "Is that Levi's boss walking over now?"

Emma turned to face Mr. Weeks.

"I'm so sorry, Emma. Is there anything at all I can do?"

Emma shook her head and Wil butted in, saying, "The community looks after its own."

Emma frowned at Wil, which caused him to look at the ground and take a slight step back. Emma knew that he was only being protective, but Mr. Weeks was just being nice and she considered Wil's actions to be quite rude.

"Do you mind if I visit you at some point in the future?" Mr. Weeks' eyes flickered nervously toward Wil. "To make sure you're okay?"

Normally Emma would have laughed and said she would be fine, but with Wil's outburst just moments before, she felt she had to be extra polite to make up for his rudeness. "That would be lovely. I'll look forward to it."

Mr. Weeks was an older man and Emma guessed

that he would have been dashingly handsome in his day. He had good bone structure with dark hair that was graying slightly at the temples. He reached into the breast pocket of his black suit and pulled out a business card. "Here's my number if you should have need of anything before then."

Emma took his card and watched Mr. Weeks walk away. There was something nice and old-worldly about the man.

"It appears I have my work cut out for me."

Emma had forgotten that Wil was standing behind her. She turned and looked into his face. "What?"

"Watching out for you. You haven't even left the graveside and already you have vultures after your farm and elderly men out to capture your heart."

By the way his jaw clenched, Emma knew that Wil was being serious for once. "Wil, you don't have to watch out for me. I'm a grown woman. Besides, I don't think that Mr. Weeks is that old, and he's rather charming." Emma loved to tease Wil whenever she could.

"Emma, Levi's only been gone five minutes – how could you even look at another man?"

Her light-hearted moment was gone, replaced with anger at Wil's response. Surely he should have known she was joking. She wanted to yell at him or tell him to mind his business. Of course she was not entertaining the slightest notion of another man in her life, but she was far too tired to explain herself; besides, why should she? "Wil, I love you like a *bruder,* but today I just can't deal with your nonsense." Emma looked at Wil's waiting buggy and then glanced back at Levi's grave. "Just take me home."

As Wil pulled the buggy away from the cemetery, the man, who had asked to buy her land, leaped toward the horse and grabbed the reins. The horse had no choice but to come to a complete halt.

"Get away from there, man! What are you doing?" Wil leaped out of the buggy and towered over the man, who meekly offered up his calling card.

"I forgot to give this to the lady. My phone number, in case she changes her mind about selling." He looked directly at Emma. "I'm offering top dollar. I'll pay more than anyone else."

Wil snatched the card from his hands. "Don't ever jump out at another buggy like that again. Do you hear me?"

The man nodded, but it didn't stop him from repeating, "I'll pay more than anyone else." The man backed away, stepping in front of another buggy before scampering off the road.

Emma put her hand over her mouth and stifled a giggle at the man's antics.

"That man is a vulture." Wil threw himself back heavily into the buggy seat and handed her the man's card. "Here, not that you'll ever need it."

"Why not?" She took the card and ran her eyes over the gold script writing.

Wil drove the horse forward and shot a glance at Emma. "You'd never sell, would you?"

"I haven't thought about it." It was true; she hadn't thought about it. There didn't seem to be any reason to sell. Even without Levi's weekly wage coming in, the monthly lease from Henry Pluver was enough to live on. She wouldn't have to go out and work. *Gott* had blessed her in that way – she knew that both Silvie and Maureen had been forced to find work when they lost their husbands.

"I don't want you to leave Levi's farm, but let me know if you ever want to sell and I'll buy it from you."

Emma smiled politely as she mumbled, *"Jah."* She didn't know if Wil could raise enough money to buy the farm. Wil fancied himself as an entrepreneur, with his hands in lots of businesses, but Levi had told her in confidence that they never made him any money. Wil owned the farm next to Emma, but just like Levi had, he leased it out to Henry Pluver to raise wheat crops while he chased income from other sources.

Chapter Two

Wealth gotten by vanity shall be diminished:
but he that gathereth by labour shall increase.
Proverbs 13:11

It had been one week since the funeral, and that was all it took – one week for Emma to find out that she was not having a *boppli*. She wondered if her life would get better; if not, she'd rather go home to be with the Lord now than carry on. She was all alone in the big *haus* that Levi had built for them; alone with memories of him and thoughts of what their life might have been.

Still in bed, Emma pulled her robe over her shoulders and watched the rain beat against the window. If Levi were alive, she'd be sipping hot coffee right now instead of trying to keep warm, alone. Levi had brought her coffee in bed every day, as she wasn't a morning person.

Levi was such a dear husband; he was one of a kind. She knew of no other Amish *mann* who looked after their *fraa* as well as Levi had. What other Amish *mann* would cook breakfast for their wife before they left for work? A smile crossed Emma's face. Mostly, it was the women who got up early to look after their men-folk.

Emma had never told anyone how good Levi was to her, just in case she was thought of as a lazy and hopeless wife. She was sure he liked doing things for her – it seemed to make him happy.

What reason did Emma have to get out of bed? She could think of a few—the chickens, along with the other animals, needed feeding. Threads, the black and white cat she was looking after for a friend, would also be hungry by now. He usually waited patiently by the hearth until he heard the rattle of the feed bucket. If it weren't for the animals relying on her, she would surely stay in bed all day.

The thought of Threads curled up on Levi's favorite chair came to her, and her heart twisted. Levi had once grumbled good-naturedly that the cat —their long term house guest—had stolen his spot, but he'd always end up scratching behind the cat's ears before sitting somewhere else. That memory warmed her for a moment.

As it was, she would stay in bed as long as she possibly could. Surely the animals wouldn't mind getting fed a little later today, seeing that it was raining. She pulled the warmth of her robe tighter around her shoulders and sank back under the covers while she listened to the rain drumming against the windowpane.

The next thing that Emma was aware of was a steady rhythmical pulse. At first she thought it was her heart beating, but quickly realized that someone was pounding on her front door.

"Emma! Emma!"

The voice was Wil's, but what was the urgency? Pulling the robe around her, she made her way down the stairs and opened the door just slightly, so he wouldn't see her in her state of undress. "Wil?"

"Emma, it's Sunday."

Wil's thick, dark hair was windswept and fell

about his face. Emma had to stop herself from reaching out to straighten it.

"Oh, is it the second Sunday already?" She hoped she didn't look too much of a fright since she'd just gotten out of bed.

"Jah, it is. Are you coming to the gathering? I don't see your buggy out front."

"Nee – I mean, I want to. Am I late?"

"I'll take you there, to save you hitching your buggy." He glanced at the bathrobe that she was doing her best to hide behind the door. "How long will it take you to get ready?"

"Nee, I don't think I can go. I haven't fed the animals yet." Emma shut her eyes tightly. Why was it so hard to carry on with simple daily chores? Well, it was morning, and she was never *gut* at mornings; maybe she'd be better later in the day.

"You get ready and I'll feed them," Wil offered.

Emma looked up into his face, groggy from still being half-asleep.

"Well? Go on," Wil told her, before he turned and strode toward the barn.

She closed the front door and headed up the stairs. Maybe the meeting would take her mind off things. *Jah,* getting out of the *haus* and talking to people would be just what she needed.

***

The first person who approached her as she got out of the buggy was Maureen. After they exchanged greetings, Maureen said, "Emma, it might be too soon for you, but Silvie and I get together with Ettie and Elsa-May and we have – sort of have – a little group." Maureen's voice lowered. "A widows' group. We don't talk about morbid things, it's not like that. We just get together as a group of friends. Do you think you'd like that?"

"I'd really love to come, *denke*." Emma wondered why this was the first time she'd heard of Maureen meeting with the other widows. Emma had thought she knew everything about Maureen – apparently she'd been wrong.

"Wednesday night at Elsa-May and Ettie's *haus* then. That's the next time we're meeting."

"Okay, I'll be there."

Wil had already gone ahead toward the crowd, which Emma was thankful for. No doubt he would have something to say about her meeting with the group of widows. *Now, he'd never have to know. It's none of his concern anyway,* Emma thought. Wil had become overprotective of her in the last week, calling in every day and trying to fix things around the *haus*, things that didn't even need fixing. He was like an overbearing older *bruder*.

As was usual at the meetings, Emma sat next to Maureen. The men and women never sat together. It was always men on one side and women on the other. Emma knew now how Maureen must have felt when she'd lost her husband. She had thought she'd understood at the time, but now she really knew what it meant. It was like having part of one's heart ripped out, leaving it bare and exposed. Emma glanced sideways at Maureen and marveled at the fact that she was always smiling.

Maureen caught her eye. "You okay?"

Emma managed a smile and a nod. The right thing to do was to carry on with life and manage the best that she could; there was no other choice.

As if reading Emma's thoughts, Maureen said, "It takes time."

"*Jah,* that's what everyone keeps telling me." Emma would have to wait and see if they were right. In a way, she didn't want to feel better. Maybe then it would seem like Levi's absence didn't affect her, and it did.

Emma found comfort in the bishop's words as he gave the talk. *Gott's* words always comforted her. Levi and she used to read the Bible together every night after dinner, even if it were just one or two verses. Since Levi had gone, she had not picked up the Bible once.

That night was the first time she'd arrived back home from a gathering without Levi. As if sensing her dread of entering an empty home, Wil said, "Are you going to be all right? Do you want me to stay for a while?"

"*Nee*, of course not. I'll be fine." Emma pursed her lips together as she realized that had become her stock standard answer for everything – 'I'll be fine.' Maybe if she said it enough times, she might even come to believe it. Emma wanted Wil to stay – she wanted someone to be with her – but she would have to face being alone eventually, and the sooner she got used to it the better off she'd be. She'd already had Wil stay with her through the young peoples' singing rather than go home earlier.

"All right. You know where I am if you need me."

Emma nodded and got out of the buggy. Wil waited until she opened the front door before he turned the buggy around and drove away.

It was dark inside the empty home. Emma promptly turned on the overhead gaslight, which was the one that gave the most illumination.

It had been a nice day and hearing the young

people singing had brightened her mood, as had Maureen's invitation.

Emma had grown too used to just having Levi's companionship and had distanced herself somewhat from the women of the community. Now, she knew that had to change.

If she was going to adapt to her new life, she needed to be more outgoing and friendly. She should have more friends, she told herself, rather than just Maureen. Maybe she would find some new friends amongst the widows.

Emma pulled her prayer *kapp* off and sat down on the couch. She unpinned her braid and unraveled it so her hair warmed up her bare neck. Without Levi's companionship, Emma would have to find something else to occupy her days. She needed something to do or she would surely go mad.

Emma's thoughts turned to Wil. He'd been good to her, and she wondered why someone so thoughtful and caring had never married. Casting her mind back, she tried to recall if he had ever courted anyone. She couldn't remember him courting, which she considered odd. He was handsome and had his own farm. Why wouldn't he have a wife by now?

At one time, Levi had mentioned that Wil was

waiting until he was financially secure – whatever that meant.

Well, maybe that's it. He's waiting for some reason that only he knows. Emma smiled. *That would be typical of Wil. Sometimes he's in his own little world.*

Emma put the kettle on the stove, deciding that she would have a hot cup of chamomile tea to help her sleep. Maureen had told her that she didn't have a full night's sleep for two months after her husband died.

Would she be better off away from this farm and this house with all the memories? But the house would still be there, and to have someone else living in the home that she'd once shared with Levi might be worse than staying in it. Maureen had also advised her not to make any major decisions for some time.

She spooned the chopped chamomile flower heads into the muslin pouch and poured the hot water over. As she let the tea steep, she thought of the bishop's words that day.

He spoke on being grateful for everything and giving thanks. Maybe in a few weeks' time she could think of things to be grateful for, but right now it was a little difficult.

Maureen had told her that time would help to heal her heart. Why couldn't she go to sleep and wake up a year later? Maybe by then she would have some happy thoughts.

It was hard not to think of Levi when everything reminded her of him. The very table and chairs where she sat had been made by Levi's *daed*. The china teacup from which she drank was part of a tea set given to her by Levi when she'd agreed to marry him.

At some point, she would have to do something with Levi's clothes. His black Bible was his only possession she would keep. After removing the muslin package from the hot water, she sipped the tea while thinking peaceful thoughts to encourage a *gut* sleep; that's what Maureen had advised her to do.

Half a cup of tea was all that she could manage. As she walked over to the sink to rinse out the teacup, she noticed the two cards that were handed to her on the day of the funeral. She placed the cup in the sink, picked up the cards and sat down.

The first card was Mr. Weeks', and it reminded Emma that he had said he would visit. The other card was from 'The Vulture,' and she hoped that she would never see him again.

It was rude of him to come to the funeral to ask her to sell her farm. According to the card, the man's name was 'Wiley McAllister.' He had to be the same man who had spoken to Levi about selling the land some time ago – Levi had given him a flat 'no', but that didn't stop the man from asking him again another two times.

Levi had told her that farming land was growing scarce, but he never wanted to sell. She would make sure that she held on to the land for him.

Besides, she reminded herself, it gave her an income. She stretched her hands over her head and yawned.

Hmm, perhaps I might sleep tonight.

With that, she rose from the table, popped the two cards into the top drawer of the kitchen cabinet, and headed up the stairs to her bedroom.

* * *

The very next day, Emma decided it best to pack Levi's things and drive them to Bessy's *haus*. Bessy took the community's unwanted items and distributed them to the various charities about the place.

Emma had five large cardboard boxes that she

had collected from the produce store. That ought to fit it all, she thought, fighting back tears as she folded his clothing into the boxes. They might help someone else. She knew she wouldn't feel better with his clothing gone from the bedroom, but it had to be done. She may as well do it now rather than later; she'd only be delaying the heartache for another day.

As she folded clothes, she heard a car outside. Looking out from her bedroom window, she saw Mr. Weeks step out of the vehicle. She threw the black suit jacket that she was holding onto the bed and hurried downstairs.

"Good morning, Mr. Weeks," she said as he stepped onto the porch.

"Good morning. I hope you don't mind me paying you a visit."

"Not at all. Please do come in." Emma stepped aside to let him into the *haus*. "Would you like a cup of tea or coffee?"

"That would be lovely, thank you."

"Sit down, please."

Mr. Weeks took a seat at the kitchen table. "The reason I'm here, besides checking that you're okay, is to tell you that I've put in an insurance claim for your husband's accident."

"I see." Emma busied herself getting the tea and

cookies. She knew that *Englischers* drank black tea and she was sure that she had some hiding in the kitchen somewhere.

He continued. "So that means you might get quite a sum of money."

"Oh, that will come in handy." Emma looked across at him.

"Maybe I shouldn't have mentioned it at all." He looked down at his hands, which were clasped on the tabletop.

"Why do you say that?"

"Levi refused his safety harness, so there's only a small chance that the insurance company will pay up. I've lodged the claim anyway. Maybe you could – well, pray about it?"

"I'll certainly do that." Emma knew that *Gott* always worked in mysterious ways, his wonders to perform. Emma wasn't quite sure what that last part meant as it ran through her head – it was part of a Scripture, she was sure of that.

"I don't know why he refused his harness." Mr. Weeks scratched his head.

"He was a very stubborn man and very sure of himself. He'd organized a lot of barn-raisings and did a lot of work at a great height; I guess he thought that he didn't need one." Emma placed the sugar cookies and a pot of tea down on the table. She glanced at Mr. Weeks' worried face. "Surely you don't hold yourself accountable?"

"In a way, I do."

"Nee, please don't. It was his decision, and he wouldn't want you to feel that way."

Mr. Weeks' eyes misted over. Emma hoped he wouldn't cry. She wasn't used to seeing men cry, and she wouldn't know what to do. "*Gott* wanted him home. It was his time to go."

Mr. Weeks nodded.

"He's in a much better place now. I know that in my heart."

"Thank you, Mrs. Kurtzler. You're very kind." Mr. Weeks took a sip of the hot tea then picked up a sugar cookie. "Will you be staying on here – on the farm?"

Why was everyone so interested in whether she was staying on the farm? Was the whole town trying to make her sell? That's certainly what it felt like. "The farm is leased, so it's enough for me to live on. I've no reason to sell." Especially if the insurance money comes through, she thought.

"I see. So you lease the whole farm? To a wheat farmer?"

"We..." She caught herself. "I mean, I lease out

all the land except the *haus,* the barn and a little plot where I grow vegetables. Henry Pluver uses it. He's an Amish man who leases a few parcels of land around the area. He's got his own farm too, but I've heard that it isn't very big."

Mr. Weeks scratched his chin. "He's Amish, you say?"

"Yes, he is."

"Pluver is an unusual name."

"I guess it is. Come to think of it, his is the only Pluver family in the community. I'm not sure of their history."

Mr. Weeks looked thoughtful as he nibbled on the sugar cookie. "Are you friendly with the Pluver family?"

"No, not especially." Emma thought about the Pluvers – the sour-faced Mrs. Pluver, the creepy son, Bob, and Mr. Pluver, who was just a typical Amish farmer. "It's certainly good news about the insurance money, if it comes through."

Mr. Weeks held up his hand. "I wouldn't go spending it just yet."

Emma smiled at the thought of going on a spending spree. She was very frugal with money, as was all her *familye*. She'd been taught from a young age to make do with what she had. She could cook and sew and had need of very little. The money would just sit somewhere in case the farm needed something or the *haus* needed repair.

"Emma?" came a voice from the front door.

"Come in and join us, Wil."

Wil walked through to the kitchen. Mr. Weeks stood and nodded his head as a greeting. Wil did the same.

Emma noticed that the two men didn't shake hands. They are probably still at odds with each other over the incident at the funeral. Emma considered that Wil had been rather rude to Mr. Weeks at the funeral when the older man had only offered her help.

As Wil sat at the table, Emma saw that his face was flushed, and she figured that he must have rushed over when he saw a strange car parked in her driveway.

There was an awkward silence and Mr. Weeks took a large gulp of tea. Wil's hostility towards Mr. Weeks was obvious, and Emma was not the only one who sensed it.

She stood. "I'll fix you some tea, Wil."

"*Denke,* Emma. So, Mr. Weeks, what brings you here today?"

"I'm visiting Mrs. Kurtzler, as I mentioned I

would. I can assure you I have no ill intentions. Levi Kurtzler was a respected member of my team and I'm sure he would want me to see that his wife has everything she needs."

Emma let out the breath that she had been holding onto. She hoped those words would put Wil's overprotectiveness to rest.

"As I told you the other day, we look after our own. I appreciate your visit but I will see that Emma has everything she needs." Wil's tone was bordering on hostile – again.

Emma nearly dropped the teapot she had just picked up. "Wil."

Wil looked at her, stony faced.

Mr. Weeks stood abruptly. "I'll be going now then, Mrs. Kurtzler. Please, you've got my number if you need anything, and we'll discuss that other matter if anything comes of it."

"Yes, thank you. I'll see you out." Emma walked Mr. Weeks to the front door. "I'm so sorry about that," she whispered.

Mr. Weeks shook his head. "Doesn't matter. It didn't bother me." He gave her a smile and a little wink before he turned and walked to his car.

Emma marched straight back to Wil, who had a

mouthful of cookie. "Wil, don't you think that was a bit rude?"

"Nee, I don't. There was only one thing he was doing here, Emma. He's attracted to you and you're a woman on your own. You have to be more careful. You can't just let people into the *haus* like that."

Emma folded her arms across her chest and looked down at him as he sat at the table eating cookies. "Well, you're in the *haus* aren't you?"

He shook his head, and his eyes turned to the ceiling. "That's different. You're like my little *schweschder*. We've been friends forever."

So that's what he thinks of me. He doesn't see me as a woman; he sees me as his little schweschder. Emma didn't know why, but she was a little disappointed to know that he thought of her in that way. Although, neither did she want the aggravation of him being attracted to her – it was far too soon for her to consider another man in her life.

Why was she so upset by his words? Maybe she was trying to make up for her loss in some way. She sat down opposite him, picked up a cookie and took a bite. They sat in silence for a moment; the only noise was that of crunching cookies.

"Before Mr. Weeks arrived, I was packing Levi's clothing into boxes."

"Do you need help?"

Emma shrugged her shoulders. She didn't know what she needed. Maybe she wanted help, and maybe she didn't. Maybe she wanted to be alone while she packed up Levi's clothes. "I'm planning to take them over to Bessy's place."

Wil took a mouthful of his tea then placed the teacup down on the table. "I'll take them to Bessy's for you."

"That would be a help. You could carry the boxes down the stairs for me too."

"Of course."

Emma was grateful for his help, but at times he was too much. Sometimes she just wanted some space. Emma's thoughts turned to Bessy. She was around the same age as Wil and she had never married either. For a moment, she wondered if they would make a match, but then Emma dismissed the idea. If they were to make a match they would've had plenty of time to get together before now. But then, who was there for Wil and who was there for Bessy? It dawned on Emma that she should be grateful that she had known real love. It was clear that many of the married people she saw about the place were not happy with their choices, and there was a handful of people in the community who remained unmarried.

Levi and she had been happy and very much in love; for that, she was thankful.

A smile flickered across her face. She had found something to be grateful for, just like the bishop had said – and to think, only days ago, she'd thought she had nothing.

Chapter Three

And God shall wipe away all tears from their eyes; and there shall be no more death, neither sorrow, nor crying, neither shall there be any more pain: for the former things are passed away.
Revelation 21:4

Maureen arrived at Emma's house to give her a ride to the widows' meeting. Emma saw her out the window, and paused to nudge Threads away from the front door with her foot. "Not now, you," she murmured as the cat twisted between her legs, batting at the hem of her dress.

Emma hurried to the buggy, holding a freshly baked pie.

"You've baked?" Maureen glanced at the plate of food Emma held in her hand.

Emma climbed into the buggy. "*Jah,* I thought I'd bring something with me."

"Well, put it in the back with my lot."

She stretched her arm to put the plate on the back seat next to two larger plates.

"I've baked a couple of things too," Maureen said.

Emma looked across at Maureen and noticed that she looked a little weary. "Are you okay, Maureen?"

"*Jah,* I'm all right. Just a little tired. I started work early this morning."

Maureen worked at a restaurant, cleaning of a morning and sometimes of an evening. "Not working tonight then, I guess?"

"*Nee.* Three days a week I work in the evenings, and six days a week in the mornings. It's odd hours, but that makes the pay better."

Maureen was in her late thirties, which was quite a bit older than Emma. She was very confident and sure of herself, except when she spoke of her late husband. It was clear to Emma that Maureen missed her husband dreadfully.

Ten minutes later, they arrived at Ettie and Elsa-May's *haus*. It was a tiny little place and it glowed like a beacon, surrounded as it was by large, dark trees.

"Looks like Silvie's here already," Maureen said as she tipped her head toward the other buggy in the drive. "You go on ahead with the food – I'll just tie up the horse."

Emma struggled with the three plates, but somehow managed to knock on the door.

"Come in, dear. Nice to have you here," Ettie said, letting Emma in.

Elsa-May came up behind Ettie and greeted Emma.

"We brought some cookies and things," Emma said, handing Ettie one of the plates.

"Ahh, denke. We won't say no to food," Elsa-May laughed, taking the other two plates from her and heading to the kitchen.

Emma hung around the doorway until Maureen came and ushered her into the living room where Silvie sat. There was no couch, which might have been more comfortable – just hard wooden chairs.

The two older widows came into the living room; Elsa-May had knitting in her hands and Ettie had needlework. Elsa-May held up the knitting, which was a soft yellow color. "I'm to be a *grossmammi* again." She offered the information to Emma. It was clear that the other ladies already knew.

"That's so exciting. How many *grosskinner* do you have?"

"I've six others, and this will make seven."

Although Emma smiled, she tried hard not to think of the fact that she had no *kinner* to remind her of Levi, and she would never have any *grosskinner* either.

Ettie leaned slightly forward. "Does that upset you, Emma?"

"*Nee,* I'm happy for Elsa-May."

The ladies all looked at her – they could see straight into her heart.

Maureen explained. "The group is here so we can tell each other our inner thoughts and feelings. What you tell us will not leave this room."

Emma looked at each lady in turn. They had their eyes fixed upon her. She could see they were all filled with love, united by the bonds of loss. "All right then. If I'm totally honest – I'm upset that I don't have *kinner*. I thought that I might be having a *boppli* and I just found out that I'm not." Tears ran down Emma's cheeks. She could feel her face contort into something ugly, but she didn't care. She cried harder.

Silvie was the closest to Emma, and she put her arms around her. "Let it all out. It's fine to cry."

The other ladies murmured in agreement with Silvie's advice. Emma put her arms around Silvie's neck and cried some more.

Ettie placed her embroidery on the floor and disappeared, returning with a handkerchief.

"*Denke,*" Emma managed to say. After a while, Emma stopped crying and blew her nose. "I'm so sorry." She looked at their concerned faces. "I feel so foolish."

"*Nee*, don't. We've all been through it. You might find you cry at odd times because you're so used to holding it all in and putting on a brave front," Silvie said.

"*Jah,* when you feel like crying, it's best to let it out," Maureen added.

"I'll have to get used to hearing that people are having *bopplis,* I suppose, and seeing couples happy. I just don't know why *Gott* had to take Levi now. Couldn't I have had a few more years with him and at least a *boppli* – or maybe two?" Emma asked.

"Who knows the mind of *Gott?*" Elsa-May said.

Ettie added, "No one does. We just have to trust Him; we're not called to understand Him."

"Anything else on your mind, Emma?" Maureen asked.

Emma managed a smile. "*Nee*, nothing else." She wanted someone else to say something. She felt as if she'd dominated the group with her problems for long enough.

"I longed for a *boppli* as well, Emma. I know how you feel," Maureen said.

Emma acknowledged Maureen's admission and smiled. It was at least *gut* to know that someone knew the pain that she was going through. "Tell me, does it get easier?"

Maureen smiled, revealing the slight gap between her two front teeth. "Oh, *jah*. It does. I find I have to keep myself busy, though. Busy with lots of things, and working helps as well."

"I find it best not to think about him at all. I got rid of everything he owned, and I put him out of my mind. Every time I think about him I still want to cry," Silvie said, tears in her eyes.

A silence fell over the group. Elsa-May clapped her hands. "Let's eat." She rose to her feet and they all followed her to the kitchen. It appeared that

Emma and Maureen were not the only ones who'd brought food. There were chocolate cookies, sugar cookies, cheesecake, chocolate fudge bars, roasted almonds and dried figs.

Ettie asked, "Everyone having meadow tea?"

Everyone said 'yes' to meadow tea with the supper. Emma followed the others' lead and sat at the table in the kitchen. Even though the chairs in the kitchen were wooden as well, they were far more comfortable than the chairs in the living room.

Emma looked around at the ladies and said, "I want to thank everyone for sharing their feelings. It makes me feel so much better. Now I don't feel so alone."

The elderly Ettie put a hand over hers briefly. "That's why we meet."

Emma picked up a chocolate chip cookie and took a bite. Silvie sat opposite Emma. She was quite young to be widowed, and Emma wondered if she had ever considered getting married again. Surely *Gott* would have someone else for her, seeing as she was such a lovely girl and so pretty. Her hair was blonde, her skin creamy and her eyes the bluest of blue that Emma had ever seen. Maureen was also attractive – a little older than Silvie, but still a very handsome woman, and she was wise and intelligent. *Surely Gott could find menner for these women,* she thought. Maybe they are like me and don't want another man.

"Emma, anytime you're feeling sad you can always come visit me. I don't live that far from you," Silvie said.

"Denke, I'll remember that."

Emma knew that Maureen and Silvie had jobs. Maybe that's what she needed. If she had something to do, perhaps it would take her mind off things.

* * *

The next day, Emma forced herself out of bed and, once she'd fed the animals, threw herself into gardening. Keeping busy was her new way of coping with life without Levi.

"There you are."

Emma looked up when she heard Wil's familiar voice. "Hello. I'm gardening."

"I can see that."

Emma stood up from her crouched position. "I'm all right, Wil. You don't have to visit me every day."

"I'm just making sure you're okay – not being hassled by vultures or anyone else."

The Amish Widow

"*Nee,* no one's been around."

"*Gut.* Well, if you have everything under control, I'll be on my way."

Emma didn't want to rely on Wil. She had to be self-sufficient if she was going to get through these next few months – everyone told her it was going to be tough. "*Denke,* Wil, for everything you've done."

Wil turned to leave. As he walked away he put a hand in the air and gave a wave.

She was comforted by the knowledge that Wil was on the farm next door. If she ever did need anything, he was only a few minutes' walk away.

Emma crouched down again with her garden fork in hand. "Where do all these weeds come from?" she asked herself out loud.

Threads moved over from the porch, tail high, and rubbed against her leg. Emma smiled faintly and reached down to stroke him. "At least someone still wants me around."

A few moments later, Emma heard a car in the driveway. She stood up and walked around to the front of the house. Rarely did she have a visit from anyone in a car. The vehicle was large and black, and she couldn't see inside as the windows were dark. The driver's-side door opened slowly, and Emma suffered pangs of anxiety when she saw 'The Vulture' emerge from the car.

Emma didn't wish to have to contend with this man again, this man who wouldn't take 'no' for an answer. She glanced up the road hoping that Wil was still around, but she could see no sign of him.

Chapter Four

Truly my soul waiteth upon God:
from him cometh my salvation.
He only is my rock and my salvation;
he is my defence; I shall not be greatly moved.
Psalm 62:1

"Mrs. Kurtzler, I hope you don't mind me visiting you."

Emma took a step back toward her *haus*. "I most certainly do. You've been told already that I am not selling. Please leave my property."

He took a step closer to her. "It's a big place for you to manage just by yourself."

Emma folded her arms and held her head up high. "Well, it's none of your concern. Anyway, I lease it out, so it's all under control."

The Vulture was not going to give up easily. He moved clear of his car and walked toward her. "Mrs. Kurtzler, if you invest the money that I pay you for the farm, I'm sure it will make you a far greater profit than a lease would." He moved another step closer, which left only four feet between them. "What we need to do is sit down and go through the figures."

Emma considered him condescending. He spoke as if she wouldn't know how to manage money just because she was a woman. "Mr... Whatever your name is, it's not all about money. I'm trying very hard to be polite to you, but I don't know how much longer I can do so. Please leave my property now, or I shall call someone and have you removed." Emma lifted up her chin some more and tried to look confident, while secretly wishing she had a telephone installed in the barn like a lot of other Amish folk did. She couldn't call someone even if she wanted to, but The Vulture didn't know that.

"An attractive woman like you shouldn't be out

here by herself – you never know what might happen."

A ripple of fear ran down Emma's spine – she was alone, and if this man got nasty she had no defenses. Out of the corner of her eye she spied the gardening fork. If he got violent, she would be forced to use it to defend herself. "Leave my property now."

"I'm just trying to be helpful. What I'm offering you is a good deal."

"Please go." Maybe she was too polite; she tried again, a little louder. "Just get in your car and go." She glared into his eyes.

He turned and walked back to his car slowly. Once he'd opened its door, he said, "My office is above the post office if you change your mind."

Emma stared him down as he got in his car and drove away. She threw her head back, let out a groan and then went inside, careful to lock the door after herself. Sitting at the kitchen table, she tried to calm herself down. *A cup of tea is what I need*, Emma thought. Once she had relaxed a little, she put the kettle on the stove. *Should I tell Wil that The Vulture came to the haus? Nee, he's already concerned enough; I don't want him coming over twice a day to watch me. Once is plenty.*

In the back of Emma's mind, she wondered why

Wil was so fast to get to her place when he saw Mr. Weeks' car, but he'd done nothing to rescue her when The Vulture appeared. Surely The Vulture's car would have passed Wil on his way home.

While she drank the hot chamomile tea, she decided to go into town and get some needlework. That would give her something with which to occupy herself. She also considered getting some sort of a weapon, something a little better than a gardening fork. Was The Vulture threatening her, talking about her being all alone, or just trying to scare her? She wasn't sure. Maybe she would look around the barn and see what she could use to defend herself.

Emma hitched the buggy for her trip into town and then had a look around the barn for a weapon of self-defense. The best she could find were a pitchfork and a spade. She put them both in the back of the buggy just in case she had any trouble on the journey to town and back.

The wool and craft shop was more crowded than Emma had ever seen it. It was as if everyone had decided to go there that day. She spotted her friend Maureen at the back of the shop. "Maureen."

"Hello, Emma. I was going to visit you later today."

"Please still come. I'd love it if you did." Seeing Maureen's smiling face always made Emma happy.

"I'll come see you in a couple of hours, if you'll be home by then."

"I'll be home. I just came here to get something to sew." Emma held a couple of things that she had chosen in the air. "Trying to keep busy and all."

Maureen smiled, revealing the familiar gap in her front teeth as she did so.

Before long, a queue formed in the shop as people waited to pay for their goods. Maureen was first in the queue; she paid for her things and left. Emma was five back from the register. The next person to be served was taking a long time, and Emma wondered whether the sales assistant was having a gossip session instead of serving the woman.

Emma impatiently shifted her weight from one foot to another, and then glanced out the window. Across the road, she saw Wil, but who was the man he was talking to? She looked a little harder and saw that the man Wil was speaking to was The Vulture.

"Next," the sales assistant shouted.

Emma looked around, but she was still three from being served. She turned again to study the two men. They were speaking to each other in a civil manner, as though they were friends. Emma frowned. *That can't be right – why would Wil be talking to that horrid man? They certainly look to be friendly, but Wil was so rude to him at the funeral. Why is he being nice to him now?*

"Next."

Emma looked up to see the bored sales assistant waiting for her to bring her items to the counter.

Once she paid for the goods and was ready to leave the shop, Emma looked out the window again, but the two men had gone. She stepped out of the store and looked both ways up the street, but there was still no sign of either man. Confused and upset at what she'd seen, she hurried back to her buggy. She passed the post office and remembered the terrible man saying his office was located above it. She stopped and stepped through the doorway that led to the upstairs offices. Ah, there it was: 'McAllister Realtor.' *I just don't like the way the man conducts business by harassing people.* She stepped back out onto the pavement.

What she needed was something to make herself feel better, and she knew just the thing. Nearly every time Emma came to town, she stopped at the specialty chocolate shop. The hand-made chocolate tasted so much better than regular store-bought candy. Emma had once tried to make her own at home, but nothing compared to the chocolate from the little store that she had found in town. She felt that she deserved a little indulgence every now and again.

After she paid for her favorite soft-centers, she decided to buy a cake for Maureen's visit. The next store she came to was a café with a bakery attached, and she wondered if she might buy a few cookies as well. Before Emma got to the front door, she happened to glance through one of the two full-length windows. It was through one of those windows that Emma saw an odd sight: Wil and The Vulture were sitting together having lunch, and they were laughing as though they were old friends.

Nee, surely not – that can't be The Vulture I see with Wil. Emma looked harder, and her first sighting was confirmed; indeed, it was the horrid little man himself. Emma continued walking past the café window, hoping that neither man would see her.

Emma strode on, quite forgetting the idea of cakes or cookies. She climbed into the buggy and drove her horse toward home.

Usually, the clip-clop of the horse's hooves soothed whatever disagreeable mood she might be in, but today her nerves were shattered beyond repair. She couldn't shake the sight of the two men talking amicably. What on earth would they have to laugh and chat about? A few days earlier, Emma had concerns of Wil's rudeness to the man, and now they appeared to be the best of friends. It didn't make sense. Emma forced the two men out of her mind and concentrated on Maureen's visit.

After Emma put the buggy away and tended to the horse, she walked out of the barn to see a gray buggy heading towards the house. She recognized it as belonging to Henry Pluver.

Emma met the buggy and noticed that Bob, Henry Pluver's adult son, was also there. Emma always felt uneasy around Bob, and Levi had told her never to let him around the *haus* if she was there by herself. Bob never talked to anyone and that unnerved many people.

"I'm sorry to hear what happened to your husband," Henry said.

"Denke."

He would only be there to discuss the lease; Emma knew that for sure and for certain. She and Levi weren't close with the Pluvers even though they were in the same community. They might not have spoken at all if it weren't for the lease. "My lawyer said that the lease is fine and can carry on as is." Well, what her lawyer had actually said was that as long as Mr. Pluver was happy to carry on as usual the lease would suffice, but since the lease was in Levi's name as well as her own, it did give Pluver an 'out' if he wanted one.

He avoided eye contact with her as much as possible when he said, "That's why I'm here. I can't carry on with the leasing of your property."

Another blow, Emma thought. It had never occurred to her that Pluver would want to stop leasing her land. That was how he derived his income, after all. What would she do now? With no money coming in, she would surely be forced to sell the farm unless she could find someone else to lease it quickly.

"Why is that? You've been leasing the land for years."

"The business is going in another direction. Anyway, I will pay you until the end of the month and that's all."

Emma felt the weight of the generations of Levi's ancestors who'd worked the farm fall heavily on her shoulders. "What prompted your decision?"

"The business is going in a different direction," he said again.

That told Emma absolutely nothing. "Is there a chance you'll change your mind?"

Bob stood beside his father, never looking at her or speaking to her once. Mr. Pluver said, "Nee, everything's set in place. I'm sorry to do it at a time like this."

Emma nodded, and Henry and Bob wasted no time in getting into their buggy and driving away.

What would she do now? She didn't even have Levi to talk things over with. She was on her own and about to lose her husband's legacy. She wondered what else could go wrong. Emma walked back to the buggy, took out the pitchfork and the spade, and placed them in the utility room of her kitchen. She was not going to be without some self-defense in her *haus* tonight. She might even keep one of the objects under her bed. Bob Pluver sent shivers up and down her spine, and so did McAllister, The Vulture.

* * *

Half an hour later, Emma was pleased to see Maureen's happy face at her door.

"So, how are you handling everything? It can't be easy with Levi gone."

Emma inhaled deeply. "I'm glad I went to Elsa-

May and Ettie's place. I think I've found new friends in them, and Silvie, of course."

Maureen remained silent and sipped her tea. "John, my *bruder,* can come help if you need anything done around the place."

"*Denke,* Maureen, but Wil's only next door. He comes over nearly every day to make sure everything's okay."

Maureen raised her eyebrows. "Does he?"

"Stop it, Maureen. Don't say it like there's something going on."

Maureen pursed her lips and leaned toward Emma. "I've always thought that he had feelings for you. I wouldn't be surprised if he's never married because he's in love with you."

"What? Don't be ridiculous. He's always been Levi's best friend and nothing more." The situation with The Vulture and Wil kept playing on Emma's mind. "Oh, I've had a dreadful day."

"Why, what's happened?"

Emma swallowed hard and braced herself to speak. "Did you see a small, balding *Englisch* man at the funeral?"

Maureen put her elbow onto the table and cradled her full face in the palm of her hand. "There were a few *Englischers*. Do you mean the one that John and I nearly ran over in the buggy?"

Emma recalled the scene of The Vulture nearly being trampled by a horse as he backed away from Wil. "Oh, was that your buggy?"

"*Jah,* we saw he'd grabbed onto Wil's horse. Who is he?"

Emma pushed her lips out. It was hard for her to talk about the farm. "He wants me to sell the farm to him."

"Nee. And he asked you at the funeral?"

Emma nodded.

Maureen's green eyes flashed. "You wouldn't sell, would you?"

"Nee. I mean, I had no reason to sell until today. Henry Pluver just came and told me he wouldn't be leasing the farm any longer. Anyway, that's not all I was going to tell you."

"What else?"

"At the funeral, Wil scolded the man and told him to leave me alone, but today when we were at the craft store I saw them across the road. They were speaking to each other, looking very friendly."

Maureen frowned and pouted her lips out in an exaggerated manner.

Emma continued, "Then later, I saw them

together in a coffee shop, having lunch. What do you think of that? They were speaking as if they were great friends."

Maureen placed her teacup back on the table and then nibbled on a cookie. "It's quite clear actually. It would appear that the two of them are in cahoots."

"Ca-what?"

"You know, in it together. Either they are trying to buy your property together or the short man has paid Wil to encourage you to sell – like a spotter's fee or something. There could be a number of scenarios."

"Nee, Wil would never do anything like that."

Maureen completely ignored Emma's comment. "Or maybe Wil wants to purchase the land and he's instructed the short man to act as his agent so you won't know it's really Wil buying it."

Emma considered what Maureen had said. "Nee, I can't see that any of those things are possible. Wil wouldn't deceive me. What reason would he have for doing that?"

"Think about it, Emma. You've a large piece of prime farmland and it joins onto Wil's property. They'd both be worth a heck of a lot more together than they would as two single farms."

Emma looked at Maureen's beady eyes. "Would they?"

Maureen nodded enthusiastically. "It's too much of a coincidence that Pluver has pulled the plug on the lease now, too. Someone's trying to force you off your land."

A chill ran down Emma's spine. She would definitely take the pitchfork up to her bedroom with her tonight. Emma recalled how Wil was always looking for opportunities to make money, but would he really try to use her to make his fortune – the widow of his best friend? She hoped it was not true.

"You were in the same friendship group as Wil and Levi growing up, weren't you?" Emma had not grown up in the area – she had met Levi at her cousin's wedding and stayed on to marry him, leaving her family and friends a hundred miles away. Although Emma had not grown up in their community, Maureen had.

"*Jah*, I was."

"Wil was trustworthy then, wasn't he?"

"*Jah*, I thought he was trustworthy, but people can change. There's something funny going on with your farm, I just know it. If something smells like a snake, it usually is a snake."

Emma nodded as she wondered what snakes smelled like.

"Oh, golly. I promised John and his *fraa* that I'd visit them for dinner. Anyway, you should tell the group about this next time we meet. They're very good at figuring things out."

"Really? I might do that. *Denke* for visiting me, Maureen." Emma rose to her feet to walk Maureen out to her buggy. "You brightened up my day."

"Come and visit me. And watch out who you trust, it sounds like someone really wants your farm."

"I will. I will on both counts – I will visit you, and I will watch who I trust."

Emma closed her front door and bolted it. She never bothered much with locks – even when she went to the stores or the gatherings she rarely locked her doors – but today she didn't feel safe. Could she trust Wil? Yesterday she would have trusted him with her life, but today she was not so certain. Her once-perfect world seemed to be growing less-so every minute. Since Levi had died, things seemed to get worse every single day.

As Emma sat down on the couch, she exhaled hard. Threads appeared at her feet, winding around her ankles. "Where were you when I needed you," she whispered, leaning down to scoop him up. The soft purring against her chest offered a flicker of comfort. "I'm going to miss you so much when you go home."

She wouldn't cook dinner tonight; she was not the slightest bit hungry. Emma set Threads beside her and pulled out the embroidery and chocolate she'd bought earlier. Although she wasn't hungry, the chocolate should sooth the sore throat she felt coming on. Emma got a sore throat every time the seasons changed. Chocolate was the only answer, and she had a lot to get through. She pulled a rug over her knees to make herself cozy.

I'll make a start on this sampler to keep myself busy. I wonder if I should ask Wil why he was talking to that man. Nee, I'll just wait and see if he says anything to me. At least she knew she wouldn't have to wait long – Wil would visit again tomorrow, just as he did every day.

Emma popped her feet up on the coffee table, smoothed out the fluffy blanket and Threads curled up beside her. She placed a soft-center strawberry chocolate into her mouth. As the chocolate melted away on her tongue, she concentrated hard on the embroidery so she wouldn't have to think about Wil and what possible reason he could have for speaking to The Vulture. Looking down at Threads, she said, "You're one of the few males I trust these days."

Threads didn't even open his eyes, but he must've heard because he started purring.

* * *

At the next widows' meeting on the Wednesday night, Maureen encouraged Emma to tell the ladies what had gone on with Wil, The Vulture, and Pluver.

After Emma had explained the whole thing, with a little emphasis on certain points from Maureen, Emma asked the group, "So what do you all think of that?"

As usual, Elsa-May was the first to speak. "Something stinks. Someone's out to diddle you, girl."

"You think so? But even if they did buy the land, I would make sure that I got a fair price. How would they diddle me?" Emma asked.

"Well, dear, perhaps they think that you don't want to sell, so they have to find devious means to get what they want. They may not diddle you financially, but they may diddle you to encourage you to sell when you don't want to." Ettie was soft-spoken, and Emma had to make a special effort to hear what she said.

The other ladies made murmurs of agreement.

"What should I do? I kind of don't feel safe with The Vulture coming to the *haus* and all, and now I'm worried about Wil." Emma chewed on the end of her fingernail.

"More tea?" Ettie picked up the fine china teapot.

Emma nodded and held the teacup toward Ettie, hoping Ettie wouldn't spill the boiling tea on her with her shaky hands. "*Denke,* Ettie."

While Ettie filled everyone's nearly empty cups, Silvie said to the group, "What should we do about it? How will we get to the bottom of things?"

Elsa-May's eyes narrowed. "You, Silvie, will go and pay The Vulture a visit and pretend that you want to buy land in the area."

Emma turned to look at Silvie thinking she would be horrified with the idea.

Instead, Silvie nodded enthusiastically. "*Jah,* and I'll say my husband and I want to buy it, so he might believe it a bit more."

Ettie added, "Wear makeup so you'll look pretty, and be sure to make eyes at him."

Emma gasped at Ettie's words. Ettie was normally so quiet and proper.

When Ettie noticed the look on Emma's face, she said, "That means to flirt with him."

"I know what it means. I'm shocked that you'd encourage Silvie to flirt," Emma said.

"It'll help her get information, Emma," Elsa-May said.

Silvie held her chin up high. "I know what to do."

Emma swung around from looking open-mouthed at Ettie, to look open-mouthed at sweet, little, blonde-haired Silvie. Was she really going to go against the *Ordnung* to wear makeup – and flirt? "Should we go against the *Ordnung?*" Emma felt in her heart she would be just as guilty if she let Silvie go ahead with the plan.

Elsa-May's loud voice boomed, "Would *Gott* want you to be homeless with no place to lay your head?"

"*Nee,* but He does say in the Bible that vengeance is His," Emma pointed out.

"Humph." Elsa-May stuck her bottom jaw out as she said, "*Gott* gave us a brain so we could use it."

"We're using a little more than our brain here,

though," Emma said. "We're using our womanly ways – would *Gott* approve of that?"

Everyone's attention was now on Emma.

"We just want to help you, Emma, that's all," Maureen told her.

"*Jah.* You're one of us now," Silvie said.

"*Gott* put you in this group with us for a reason," Elsa-May said. "Besides, the *Ordnung* changes all the time. The bishop's allowing some people tractors now, and others can have computers for their businesses. Think of it like this: we're just ahead of our time, and *Gott* is not constrained by time; He is eternal."

Ettie chimed in, "She's right, Emma, and we're not hurting anyone; we're just trying to protect you."

The others nodded and continued looking at Emma. She could feel everyone's love and concern. Being protected was just what she needed right now – visions of her pitchfork and spade came to mind. "All right then. *Denke.* I didn't mean to sound ungrateful. I'm very thankful that you all want to help."

"Okay, we'll call it 'Operation Vulture Takedown'," Elsa-May said as she pulled out a yellow notepad and began to write.

Silvie giggled while Emma wondered what she had just agreed to.

Chapter Five

And he said unto me, My grace is sufficient for thee: for my strength is made perfect in weakness. Most gladly therefore will I rather glory in my infirmities, that the power of Christ may rest upon me.
2 Corinthians 12:9

'Operation Vulture Takedown' was to begin tomorrow, according to the plan on Elsa-May's notepad. The first step was for Silvie to visit The Vulture's office, flirt a little and see what she could find out.

Emma stepped out of Maureen's buggy and thanked her for driving her to Elsa-May and Ettie's *haus* for the widows' meeting. Emma was grateful to have some new friends who cared about what happened to her and her farmland.

She stood on her doorstep and waved goodbye to Maureen as the buggy trotted up the driveway. She was glad to be home – while she was lonely sometimes, at least it was a place where she felt safe.

Although she was happy to be back at the farm, it was late at night and Emma hated coming home to a cold, dark *haus*. Next time she would leave a light on. She turned on the gas lantern just inside the front door followed by the main gas light in the center of the living room.

As the warm glow filled the room, Threads appeared from the shadows, his tail curling around her leg. "Missed me, did you?" she said softly, reaching down to scratch behind his ears. The gentle purr that followed was a balm to the chill in the air—and in her heart.

In the kitchen, she boiled some water so she could take a hot water bottle to bed with her. Maybe she would also sip some lemon tea. Emma didn't think she'd fall asleep; normally she found it hard enough, but tonight, with all the surprises at the widows' meeting, she was sure that she'd be awake for many hours yet.

Emma had passed Wil's *haus* on the way back in Maureen's buggy, and saw that it was cloaked in darkness. Never being out this late, Emma didn't know if that was unusual for him or not. Farmers usually go to bed early, but Wil was not a farmer and Emma was not really sure how he made his money. Maybe he lived on the lease money from his farm as she did.

She filled up her hot water bottle and waited for the iron kettle to boil once more for her lemon tea. Emma hugged the hot water bottle as she waited. What would Levi think of all this intrigue? *He would be glad I've made some new friends, I guess.*

With lemon tea in hand and hugging her hot water bottle, Emma made her way up the stairs to her bedroom. She set the tea on her nightstand, placed the hot water bottle in the bed and went back downstairs to fetch her weapons. She remembered she had a hammer in the utility room – that would save her carrying the big pitchfork upstairs. Emma found the hammer, carried it back to her room and placed it under her bed. She sent up a quick prayer to *Gott* asking Him to protect her through the night.

When she returned, Threads was already curled up on the end of the bed, blinking at her sleepily. "You've made yourself comfortable, I see." She gently shifted him to one side as she climbed in. He resettled, this time resting against her feet like a furry little feet-warmer.

Emma was conscious of the space on the other side of her bed – that which had once been filled now lay empty. She still kept to her half of the bed even though she could have slept in the middle. Somehow it felt right to stay sleeping on the same side. While she sat drinking the tea, she moved the hot water bottle a little further under the blankets.

How did Maureen and Silvie cope, living alone? They still lived in the houses they'd lived in with their husbands and they seemed to manage all right. Maureen had her *bruder* to help her with things, but Emma was not sure who helped Silvie.

* * *

That night, Emma had a troubled sleep. Every time she nodded off, she woke after only a few minutes. She'd tossed and turned due to the bad dream that The Vulture was chasing her away from her *haus* and she couldn't find her hammer. Emma woke with her heart racing and her body covered in sweat.

She sat up in bed and noticed the teacup on the floor, realizing that she'd left half a cup of tea in it

The Amish Widow

from the night before which was now spilled all over the floor. She must have knocked it over in her sleep. Emma slumped back under the covers. Somehow she felt safer in the daylight, and she managed to drag herself out of bed.

Threads hopped off the bed with a thud, stretching his legs before padding toward the door. "You had a better night than I did," she muttered, following him downstairs.

Elsa-May's plan was that they would all meet at her *haus* again at three o'clock. Hopefully by then Silvie would have gleaned some information from Mr. McAllister, The Vulture.

As Emma made herself breakfast, she looked down at the floorboards. They needed cleaning, as did the rest of the *haus*. It had been sorely neglected since Levi had gone. She decided that she would spend the first part of the day cleaning the *haus*, starting with the kitchen.

On hearing a buggy approach, Emma dried her hands and went to the front door. It was Wil, which surprised her – he usually walked to visit since he lived so close.

"Hello, Wil."

"I'm just on my way into town. Do you need anything?"

"*Nee.*" Emma had to stop herself from saying that she had been there yesterday. "*Nee, denke.* I'm stocked up with all I'll need for a while."

Wil got out of his buggy and walked toward her. "Well, why don't you come somewhere with me?"

Emma looked up at the handsome Wil. If she were ready for another man, she would have been delighted to be asked to go somewhere with him. But as it was, the timing was totally off. "Why?"

"It's not *gut* for you to stay in the *haus* by yourself all the time."

"I visited yesterday; I had dinner last night at Elsa-May and Ettie's. I have been out."

Wil laughed. "You had dinner with Elsa-May and Ettie?"

"What's so funny?"

"Nothing at all. They are a funny pair and make me laugh, that's all. I'm not being disrespectful."

Emma knew what he meant. They were a couple of funny old dears.

He touched her shoulder lightly. "Come on Emma – come on a picnic with me."

Emma hoped that Wil was not starting to like her as more than a friend. It was far too soon for her to entertain thoughts of another *mann*. Surely he can't be interested in me; nee, surely not, but he has been over here an awful lot. Maybe it's just because he was such a *gut* friend of Levi's he thinks he has to keep an eye on me, Emma thought. "I can't, I've got to..."

"Got to what?" Wil smiled widely and laid his hands casually on his hips.

"Clean the *haus*. It's in a dreadful state."

"A day will make no difference at all. Do it tomorrow. Let's go on a picnic."

Emma shook her head. "It wouldn't look right if someone saw us out together. I mean, if someone saw me enjoying myself." *Whoops, I've just admitted that I would enjoy myself with him. I hope he didn't notice what I said.*

"Just because Levi died doesn't mean you have to lock yourself up forever. Levi wouldn't have wanted that. He would want you to be happy. How about a compromise?"

Emma raised her eyebrows. She was beginning to like the sound of leaving the cleaning until the next day, but she had to be at Elsa-May's at three o'clock; after all, that's what the plan was, and she was not about to go against the plan.

"How about we go somewhere we won't be seen? That way we won't be gossiped about," Wil said, in a half mocking tone.

Emma was wavering; maybe she would enjoy a picnic. "I'd have to be back well before three."

"We can do that easily."

Emma thought of the floorboards. They didn't look that poorly – maybe another day wouldn't matter. "Don't you have to go into town, Wil?"

"I can do that later, or do it tomorrow. You stay right here and I'll pick you up in ten minutes. I'll go home and pack us a hamper."

"Okay, I'll bring some cheesecake."

Ten minutes would be enough time for Emma to sweep the floor and stave off her guilt for not giving it and the rest of the *haus* a thorough cleaning.

Emma wondered whether she was doing the right thing. Maybe she should've put the picnic off until tomorrow, and that way she would have had more information about the whole Vulture situation. Now, she'd have to hold her tongue about seeing Wil speaking to McAllister.

Half an hour later, they sat on a grassy hill overlooking a meadow. Emma considered that if she had been there with Levi it would have been very romantic. She had met Wil briefly before she had met Levi and they had gotten on very well together, but then Levi burst onto the scene and swept her off her feet. The bishop's wife, Mary, had once told her in confidence that Emma was the only girl that Wil had ever been interested in, but by then she was betrothed to Levi, and happily so.

"So what is it that you do for a living anyway, Wil? I've never really known."

Wil took a mouthful of cider and as he placed the glass back on the blanket, he said, "Quite a few things. It's too hard to explain."

"Because I'm a woman?"

Wil smiled and looked at Emma. "Nee, I didn't mean that."

Emma loved the way that Wil smiled, but she had to fight her attraction to him. It was far too soon to let herself think loving thoughts toward him. "I don't see why it would be hard to explain what you do." Normally Emma wouldn't push a point so far, but she had to find out what was going on. Why was he trying to hide what he did for his money?

"I lease the farm to Henry Pluver, as you know, and apart from that I have a few investments. Nothing to speak of, really. Then I have the inventions I work on."

Emma didn't know what more she could ask without him getting suspicious.

After talking and eating a lot of food, Emma was no closer to finding out why Wil had been speaking with Mr. McAllister. Maybe she should just ask him straight out. *Is he behind all this fuss of someone trying to force me off my land? Anyway, what was the purpose of this picnic? Maybe he's keen on me. That must be the answer. If what the bishop's wife said was true, maybe with Levi gone he wants to court me. But surely he would wait a respectable amount of time and not rush things,* she thought.

"We'd better get you home." Wil stood up and held out his hand. Emma looked at his powerful outstretched arm. Of course she wanted to be held in those strong arms of his. Was it loneliness that led her to want to be held in a *mann's* arms once more, to feel them around her waist? She had always felt safe when Levi put his arms around her. Maybe she just longed for that feeling of safety once more.

She put her hand in his, and he helped her to her feet. She stumbled a little as the leg she had been sitting on had gone to sleep. He reached an arm behind her back and caught her. She could have easily pulled away, but instead she looked up into his deep brown eyes and saw his gaze slowly move to her mouth before he pulled himself away.

"I'm sorry, Emma. I... Are you all right?"

"My leg's gone to sleep."

"Sit for a while with your leg outstretched while

I pack the buggy." He helped her sit back down on the blanket.

Emma sat looking out over the fields. She was upset with herself that she was not the one to pull away first. What would Levi have thought of her? He had only just gone and she was already craving another man's touch.

Even though she was mad with herself, she couldn't stop wondering what would have happened if she pressed her body into him and touched her lips to his. She remembered that Levi once joked that Wil never married because he was in love with her. Surely he was just teasing, but that, coupled with what the bishop's *fraa* had told her years ago, gave Emma something to think about.

Maybe he'd had a little crush on her a long time ago, but even if Wil was in love with her, he was not the kind of man to move in so quickly after his best friend's departure. That led her to another thought – if he had her best interests at heart, surely he wouldn't be deceiving her regarding her property. For all the time she had spent with Wil today, she was none the wiser of his motives regarding his possible interest in her or his talking to McAllister.

Once Wil had finished packing the buggy, he returned to crouch beside her. "Better now?"

Emma moved her leg. "*Jah,* better."

"Well, bring the blanket and let's go."

Ah, Emma thought, he's not going to risk giving me his hand. He does not want to be close to me again. Emma bundled up the blanket and placed it in the back of Wil's buggy. All the way back to her place, she contemplated asking him about The Vulture, but thought she was best to discuss it with the widows' society before she did or said anything.

As they drew closer to Emma's home, she saw three buggies pulling away from her drive. Emma was immediately worried, but tried not to act like it in front of Wil. "Looks like I've had visitors."

There was one buggy in her driveway when she pulled up. As soon as Emma saw the distinctive brown and white markings of the bishop's horse, she knew she could relax. The bishop's wife, Mary, was standing on her porch.

Wil stopped the buggy and Emma walked toward Mary. "Mary, it's nice of you to visit."

"I was just going. A few of the ladies have given your *haus* a *gut* cleaning and we've got a week's worth of food for you." She took Emma's hand. "You won't have to do anything for a whole week." She pulled Emma forward and gave her a kiss that she always gave people, calling it a 'holy kiss.'

Emma turned to look at Wil, who was still in his buggy. "You knew about this?"

"Of course. I was instructed to get you away from here for a few hours."

She turned back to Mary. *"Denke* so much, and thank the other ladies. This is just *wunderbaar."*

"I'll be on my way, then." Mary bustled over to her buggy.

"I'll go too, Emma." Wil tipped his hat and drove back up the driveway.

Emma felt a little foolish for thinking that Wil liked her, and that was the reason he had invited her on a picnic. Wil was simply getting her out of the *haus* so the ladies could surprise her. What a fool she would have been if she had leaned into his hard body, thinking that he was keen on her. She would have to be more careful in the future. Missing Levi's strong arms around her had left her vulnerable to another man's touch. She wouldn't let that happen again.

Emma pushed her front door open, realizing she must have left the door unlocked. She couldn't do that again, not with The Vulture hanging around, but was certainly nice to come home to a clean *haus*. Emma put her hand to her mouth and giggled as she wondered if any of the ladies had seen the hammer under her bed.

Emma looked around at her spotless home, thankful that she had run the broom over the floor before she left, otherwise what would the women have thought of her housekeeping skills?

Chapter Six

*While the earth remaineth, seedtime and harvest,
and cold and heat, and summer and winter,
and day and night shall not cease.*
Genesis 8:22

On the dot of three, Emma pulled up to Elsa-May and Ettie's *haus* as arranged. Maureen was already there, and they all had to wait fifteen minutes for Silvie to arrive.

"Sorry I'm late," Silvie said.

"Come in." Elsa-May pulled on Silvie's arm and hurried her to the chairs where the other ladies waited eagerly.

Silvie looked very pretty with the subtle makeup. Her face didn't look painted; her skin looked smooth, her lips very glossy and a little darker than normal. Her normally pale lashes were dark and very long, which accentuated her beautiful, clear blue eyes.

"Well, I asked Mr. McAllister if he had a farm for sale. He showed me brochures of farm land and I said that I wanted land close – in a ten minute radius – by buggy."

"Go on," Ettie said as she sat on the edge of the old timber chair.

"He said he could have a very large piece of land coming up, but he already had a buyer for it."

Ettie gasped and covered her mouth. "Emma, he already has a buyer for your land."

"It could be Wil," Maureen said.

Emma lowered her head and rested it in her hands.

Elsa-May lifted up her hands to quiet everybody. "We can't be sure, though. This is all hearsay."

Ettie nodded. "Quite right. What else, Silvie?"

"He stepped out of the office to take a phone call in private. So I dashed to the front of his desk and looked in his top drawer and found this." Silvie opened her palm to reveal a key. On the key was a tag, which said, 'Spare Office Key.'

The Amish Widow

Elsa-May clapped her hands. "Well done, Silvie, well done."

Emma stared at the key in disbelief. "What can we do with that?"

Elsa-May pointed at her. "You, Emma, will go there tonight – no, not tonight. Friday night. You will go into his office and look through his files, his messages – anything you can find until you know what's going on."

Maureen interrupted. "Tomorrow night is Friday night."

"So it is. Well, you must go tomorrow night." Elsa-May was insistent.

Emma clutched at her throat. "Isn't that against the law? I don't want to go to jail."

Ettie leaned forward. "It's breaking and entering. No, wait – it may not be breaking if you have a key. But if you have stolen the key, I'd say it's still breaking, and it's most certainly entering."

Emma jumped to her feet. "This is absurd – I can't do it. I can't!"

"Jah, you can. I'll come with you," Maureen said. "There's something going on, Emma, and you have to find out what it is. Don't you want to know if you can trust Wil or not?"

Emma thought back to the romantic picnic she

had just had with Wil. What if she had kissed him or something awful, only to find out he was not to be trusted? *"Jah,* but *Gott* reveals all things in time."

"How much time do you have, though, Emma? With Pluver not renewing his lease? Maybe this is an answer to prayer – *Gott* gave you a brain to use and two feet. He didn't say that He'll work everything out and for us to sit on our bottom, did He?" Elsa-May said in her usual booming voice.

Emma considered how hard Levi's *familye* had worked on the farm for the past few hundred years. Now what was to become of it if she sat on her hands and did nothing? She didn't want to be the one to lose Levi's farm to strangers or land developers. Emma exhaled a large breath. "Okay, I'll do it." She nibbled on a fingernail, hoping that she wouldn't regret the decision she had just made.

Ettie said nothing, but all eyes were on her as she feebly walked across the room to a cupboard. She slowly opened the cupboard door and pulled out a plastic bag, tipping the contents on the floor. Out fell three pairs of thin rubber gloves, a flashlight, three black ski masks and a pocketknife. Crouching over the contents, Ettie looked up at Maureen and Emma. "You both going?" They each nodded and Ettie passed the equipment to them.

They only had a day to organize the break-in. Maureen met Emma at her farm the next morning to go over the finer details.

"How should we get there? We can't really clip-clop down the street with all the buggy lights flashing in the dark and then park outside his office. If anything should happen, people would surely remember a buggy parked outside," Emma said.

"Quite right. We'll leave from my *haus* by taxi, have the taxi take us to the other end of town, and then walk the rest of the way."

Emma nodded. It seemed a reasonable plan.

When the time came for Emma to go to Maureen's place in order to get a taxi into town, she just wanted the whole thing over with. She'd spent all night tossing and turning in nervous anxiety. Would she really find something in The Vulture's office that would make sense of it all? Was Wil her friend or her foe? Why did Mr. Pluver suddenly pull out of the lease after years farming the land? Had Pluver pulled out, or tried to pull out, of Wil's lease as well? Emma made a mental note to find that out. Was it all a coincidence or was there some larger conspiracy happening, and if there was, would they find out from snooping in The Vulture's office?

As planned, they had the taxi drop them at the

top of town. They walked down the street dressed in their black coats, black stockings and black boots. Thankfully, it was cold so they didn't draw too much attention from having their coats wrapped around themselves. Instead of their white prayer *kapps,* they had their black over-bonnets on.

"Don't look so worried," Maureen whispered. "You need to look as if you don't have a care in the world and you're just taking a stroll in the cool night air."

Emma nodded and forced a carefree expression on her face.

"That's better. Now stay like that until we get there – just a couple of blocks to go."

The streets weren't crowded. A few restaurants were open and a handful of people wandered to and fro. No one paid them much attention. As they got to the block where the office was located, Maureen looked around. The entrance to the upstairs offices was set into the building, and they came to a locked door that protected the stairwell.

Maureen looked down at the key. "Oh no, we don't have a key for this door. Silvie said it was the key to the office, not the key to the downstairs door."

"We should try it anyway, Maureen." Maureen was about to put the key in the lock when Emma spoke again. "Wait. We must put the gloves on and wipe the key, too." Emma drew two sets of gloves out from inside the front of her dress. When they had both pulled them on, Maureen inserted the key in the lock and turned it.

To their amazement, it unlocked the door. "Well, I hope it works on the one upstairs as well," Maureen said.

Emma gave Maureen a little shove. "Quick, let's just get in before someone sees us."

They both slipped through the door and were faced with a well-lit staircase.

"Silvie said it was just one flight up." Maureen made her way up the stairs and Emma followed close behind, grateful that she had Maureen to lead the way. When they reached the top of the stairs, they saw three office doors. The closest one to them belonged to an accountant, the second was a financial advisor and the one farthest away had 'McAllister' written on it.

"Come on," Maureen whispered over her shoulder.

"I'm right behind you."

Maureen put the key in the lock, and the slight pressure on the door pushed it wide open. She swung around to Emma. "It was unlocked."

"He must have forgotten to lock it," Emma whispered back.

When they were both inside the office, Maureen closed the door behind them and turned on the flashlight.

"Careful to keep it away from the window. Keep it down low." Emma knew nothing of breaking into a place, but it made sense to keep the light away from the window. They didn't need any witnesses.

Maureen gave the flashlight a couple of sharp hits. "We should've put some new batteries in this thing."

"Here, give it to me." Emma wanted to read the papers that were sprawled across his desk. She picked up the first stack of papers stapled together and Maureen peered over her shoulder. She read names on the paper out loud and then said, "I don't know these people, do you?"

"Nee."

Emma leaned over the desk and searched the papers some more. The name Levi Kurtzler caught her eye. She snatched up the paper. "Look, Maureen, Levi's name."

Maureen leaned closer. "Looks like a contract for the sale of your land, but was the land in your name as well as Levi's?"

"Jah, Levi had the land put into my name as well, as soon as we married."

Maureen took the flashlight from her and had a closer look. "Weird. Anything else?"

"Here, shine the light on this one," Emma instructed.

Maureen shone the light on the papers and they both looked at each other as soon as they saw the names: Emma and Levi Kurtzler. "It looks like it's a contract for the sale of my land." Emma looked into Maureen's face. "I never ordered a contract."

"Take it with you, and let's keep looking."

It was hard for Emma to look since there was only one flashlight and Maureen was holding it. Emma moved closer to the window, hoping to read under the dim light filtering in from a street lamp. As she made her way behind the desk toward the window, she caught her foot on something and tripped over, letting out a squeal on her way down.

"Hush, Emma." Maureen turned the flashlight toward Emma's face, and it was then that the light lit up something large on the floor next to her.

Emma gasped, jumped to her feet and ran to stand behind Maureen, who trembled as she held the flashlight with both hands. "I think it's a person."

"Is it? Is it a person?" Emma asked.

Maureen took a step closer and touched the lump on the floor with her foot. There was no reaction. She reached out, moving the flashlight closer to the figure. The light shone on a face. Maureen gasped. *"Jah,* it's a person, but I think they're dead."

Chapter Seven

And now abideth faith, hope, charity, these three;
but the greatest of these is charity.
1 Corinthians 13:13

"Quick, Maureen, we have to check to see if he's still alive."

Maureen was speechless and stood as still as a statue.

Emma snatched the flashlight from Maureen's hands and shone the light on the face of the body once more, only to see that it was Henry Pluver. Through her plastic gloves, she could tell that his neck had no pulse. She checked his wrist as well, although she imagined that the neck would be the better source of information. "He's dead, for sure. And it's Henry Pluver."

Maureen gasped. "What will we do?"

"Get out of here, of course. Then we'll call the police."

Emma pushed the contract for her property down the front of her dress, grabbed Maureen's arm and hurried her outside the building. "Now remember Maureen, we have to walk up the street as if we're having a nice stroll and nothing more."

Maureen's eyes were wide, like saucers.

"Well, maybe just pull your bonnet down." Emma adjusted Maureen's bonnet so it hid the majority of her face.

They got in a taxi and went straight to Elsa-May's *haus*.

"We should call the cops and let them know," was Elsa-May's first response when she heard the news.

"Shall I go and call them from the public phone down on the corner?" Emma offered.

Elsa-May shook her head. "*Nee,* I'll call them from my cell phone."

"Your what?" Emma nearly choked. The Amish were not to have technology such as phones. Some had phones in their barns, and some had a telephone in a shanty outside their *haus,* but no one had a cell phone, at least no one that she knew of – until now.

"Cell phone. I just use it for emergencies such as these."

Did she just say emergencies 'such as these'? How many dead bodies has she had to call the police about? Emma realized her mouth was open very wide as she looked at the elderly lady in disbelief. "How do you even know how to use a cell phone?"

Elsa-May tipped her head slightly to the side. "Easy; it came with instructions."

"Elsa-May, we're not supposed to have the outside world coming into the home," Emma said, referencing the unwritten rules of the *Ordnung*.

"I'll use it outside then."

Emma was too flustered to argue. "Well, what will you say to them?"

"I'll say there's a body in an office in town." Elsa-May pressed a button on her cell.

Ettie spoke up. "Why don't we just wait until they discover it in the morning? Emma can call there just after nine. By then the place will be swarming with cops and she can gather information. Maybe get friendly with one of the cops."

Elsa-May was silent for a time. "You know, Ettie, I think you've just had your first good idea."

Emma looked at Ettie; she wasn't sure if what Elsa-May said to her *schweschder* was a compliment, but by the look on Ettie's face she had certainly taken it as one.

"Wait, I have to go back there?" Emma thought the idea a bad one.

"Of course you do. A man's been killed just after telling you he can't lease your land anymore and you find a contract for the sale of your farm. You have to go back there." Elsa-May switched off her cell phone and placed it back in the sideboard drawer. "What was he doing in The Vulture's office? You need to find all these things out."

Ettie touched Emma lightly on her arm. *"Jah,* dear. You have to go back there and get all the information you can."

"What will I say that I'm doing there?" Emma swallowed hard.

Maureen spoke up, "You could say that you're there to speak to Mr. McAllister about your farm. Say that you're thinking of selling and you want to talk it over with him."

"I'm a little scared. What if someone saw us there?" Emma asked.

Ettie shook her head. "*Nee,* don't worry about it. No one would have seen you. Besides, you didn't kill him, did you?"

Emma shook her head.

Elsa-May said, "See, nothing to worry about. Anyway, all Amish look the same to the *Englischers.* If someone saw a couple of Amish ladies, just don't say it was you. They can't prove anything. Ettie, hitch the buggy and take these two girls home – they look like they need a *gut* night's sleep."

"*Jah,* Elsa-May."

Emma was concerned by the late hour. "*Nee,* we'll get a taxi."

"*Nee,* it's no problem. I'll be two minutes." Ettie left the three women in the *haus* and went to the barn.

"I should help her," Maureen said as she walked out the front door.

"Elsa-May, sometimes I feel that you've been involved in this sort of thing before, with the flashlight, the rubber gloves and all."

"Let's just say we look after our own." She gave Emma a wink. "We'll get to the bottom of this mess, don't you worry."

Emma studied the capable old lady. Somehow she believed her words, but Emma was worried about exactly what they would uncover. She hoped that Wil had nothing to do with whatever was going on.

Chapter Eight

And the peace of God, which passeth all understanding, shall keep your hearts and minds through Christ Jesus.
Philippians 4:7

It was just as Ettie had said it would be. The place was crawling with police when Emma arrived there at nine the next morning. She walked up the stairs and found that The Vulture's office had police tape across the door. People in white coats were brushing things; Emma assumed they were looking for prints.

"Can I help you with something?"

Emma turned to see a solidly-built man. His appearance was such that Emma immediately recognized him to be a policeman or perhaps some sort of detective since he was wearing plain clothing. "I'm looking for Mr. McAllister."

"He's not here."

"What's happened in there?" Emma pointed toward the office. As she did so, she noticed a girl in the corridor crying.

"The forensics team is combing the office."

Emma gasped in a suitable manner. "Forensics? Did someone die?"

The detective studied Emma carefully. "I'm afraid so. I stationed someone on the door downstairs – how did you get up here?"

"I didn't see anyone down there. I just walked up. So, Mr. McAllister died?"

"No, it wasn't McAllister. It was someone else, but we can't release the name until we inform the family." The detective pulled a small notepad and pen from his pocket. "And what's your name?"

"My name is Emma Kurtzler." Emma lowered her voice. "Is that girl all right?"

"She's Mr. McAllister's secretary. She's the one

who called us. We've got a policewoman on the way to interview – uh, to look after her."

Emma couldn't take her eyes off the young girl, whom she guessed to be in her early twenties at the very most.

"Simpson, can you take Liza Weeks downstairs?"

A uniformed police officer stepped out of the office and guided the girl down the stairs.

The detective turned his attention back to Emma. "And what business do you have here?"

"Mr. McAllister has asked me a couple of times if I want to sell my property. I've just come here to talk about it."

"Was he expecting you?"

"No, he wasn't. I just thought I'd stop by. He gave me his card, see?" Emma pulled out The Vulture's business card and tried to think quickly. How could she possibly get some information out of the detective? "How did the man die? I assume it was a man?"

"Yes, it was. We think it was foul play, but it's too early to tell."

"You mean like murder?"

The detective nodded and turned his attention back to his small notepad. "And where can you be reached? Do you have a phone number?"

"I don't have a phone at all."

"What's your address?"

After she rattled off her address, she asked the detective, "Do you know where Mr. McAllister is?"

"No, I don't. I will need to ask you some questions later." He looked her in the eyes and leaned forward. "Don't leave town."

"Me?" Emma's hand flew to her throat. "Why would you need to ask me questions?"

"I can tell you that the man who was killed was an Amish man. You turn up here today first thing, and you're Amish – maybe there's a connection." The detective rubbed his chin.

"He was an Amish man?" Emma tried to act distressed. "That's awful."

"Yes, any murder is awful."

Emma nibbled on a fingernail as she always did when she was nervous. "I might know him, then, if he's from around here."

"I suspected you might."

Emma took two steps back. "Well, I'll leave you to it."

The detective looked at his notepad and repeated her address.

"That's correct," she said before she turned and walked away. When she got out onto the sidewalk, she tried to steady her thumping heart. That had not gone very well. She was sure she was a suspect now, from turning up like that first thing. Ettie would be upset to find out that her first good idea had not been a good idea at all.

Emma went straight home without speaking to any of the widows. They hadn't exactly given her the best guidance, since she was now most likely the main suspect. As soon as Emma put her foot on her porch, she noticed that Wil was walking down the road directly to her house.

Before she could even knock the mud off her boots, Threads appeared on the porch, stretching and letting out a long meow. "At least you're happy to see me," Emma whispered, bending to give him a quick pat before turning her attention to Wil.

"Hello, Wil."

"Hi, Emma. You're out and about early this morning, aren't you?"

"I've just been into town, to McAllister's office, but I didn't see him because the police were there."

Wil stopped still. "What for?"

"It seems that someone was murdered in his office."

Wil scratched his chin. "Who was it?"

"They wouldn't tell me the name, but they did say it was an Amish man."

"Really? I wonder who it could have been. Murdered, did you say?"

"Jah, they think it's murder, but the detective I was talking to said it was too early to know for sure. Let's sit in the kitchen."

Once they were both seated at the kitchen table, Wil spoke again. "What did McAllister say about it?"

"Like I said, I didn't see him. I don't know if the police even know where he is. The detective is coming here later to ask me some questions."

Wil reached out and grabbed Emma's hand. "You? Why's he coming to ask you questions?"

Emma was a little shocked at his touch but left her hand where it was. "The man who was murdered was Amish and I went there this morning so they think that there's a connection."

He let go of her hand and threw back his head. "Nonsense, there's hundreds of Amish in town every day."

"I suppose they have to follow every lead." Emma nibbled on her fingernail.

"That's nonsense." Wil shook his head. "Why

did you go to see McAllister anyway? Have you changed your mind about selling?"

"*Nee*, not really. I just wanted more information from him. Maybe find out how much it's worth." *He does seem concerned about me selling*, Emma thought.

"I'll stay with you until the detective comes."

Emma shook her head. "That's not necessary, Wil."

"*Jah*, I think it is necessary. You're a woman alone, Emma, and I'll not have you bullied." Wil was insistent.

"He's a policeman. I don't think that he'd bully me."

"You can't be too careful with these things. You need someone to protect you now that …" Wil looked away from Emma's face.

"It's all right, you can say it. Now that Levi's gone."

Wil looked into her face once more. "He would've wanted me to look after you."

"*Denke*, Wil."

Two hours later, a police car pulled up. Emma hoped that no one in the community would see the police car in front of her *haus*, otherwise she would have to answer too many questions.

The detective got out of the car and looked up at Emma and Wil, who were standing outside the front door. Emma noticed that there was a uniformed policeman in the driver's seat who stayed in the car.

"Hello, Mrs. Kurtzler." The detective looked up at Wil. "You Mr. Kurtzler?"

"No, I'm not. Mr. Kurtzler is deceased."

The detective stood in front of Wil, and Emma noticed they were exactly the same height.

"Oh, I see. Then who would you be?" the detective asked in an unpleasant, blunt tone.

"William Jacobson. I'm Mrs. Kurtzler's neighbor and good friend."

Emma sensed tension between the two men. "Come inside, Mr. – oh, I don't think I got your name this morning."

"It's Detective Crowley."

Once they were inside Emma showed him to the kitchen table so they could sit. "Would you like a cup of tea or a cup of coffee, perhaps?"

"No." He looked at Wil. "Would you excuse us? I'd like to ask Mrs. Kurtzler some questions in private."

Wil pulled out a chair and sat at the table opposite the detective. "No, if you don't mind, I'll stay."

The Amish Widow

The detective clasped his hands on the table. "It would be better if you didn't."

Wil leaned slightly toward the detective. "It might be better if Mrs. Kurtzler got a lawyer – then you wouldn't get your answers straight away. If I stay, however, I'm sure Mrs. Kurtzler would agree to answer your questions right now." The two men continued to glare at each other.

The detective was the first to look away. "You can stay then, as long as you keep silent."

The detective took a small notepad and pen out of his pocket. He noisily clicked the end of his pen and turned to look at Emma, who was rattling around making tea. "I said no tea for me, Mrs. Kurtzler."

"I'm just getting some for myself and Wil. I can still answer your questions while I'm making it."

The detective sat with his back very straight and said, "The man who was murdered was Henry Pluver."

"No, not Henry," boomed Wil.

The detective looked directly at Wil. "You know him?"

"Yes, of course I do. I just saw him the other day. He leases my farm right next door, and he leases Mrs. Kurtzler's farm too."

"He does?" The detective turned to Mrs. Kurtzler.

Emma nodded. "That's right. Oh, I need to sit. It's so unexpected." Emma abandoned the idea of making tea and tried to look suitably shocked and shaken.

Wil scratched his head. "I don't think we've ever had a murder within the community."

"Did Henry know Mr. McAllister?" Emma hoped it was a good time for her to start asking questions. Maybe it was a good idea to have Wil there after all.

"We'll know more of that soon. How long have you been widowed, Mrs. Kurtzler?"

"Just weeks," Wil answered on her behalf.

"I'm sorry to hear that." The detective's response showed no hint of sincerity.

Emma looked into her lap and nodded slightly.

The detective scratched something in his notepad while he asked, "And how long has Mr. Pluver been leasing your farms?"

"A good five years, I'd say." Emma got in quickly so Wil wouldn't answer all the questions. The detective had come to speak to her after all, and Emma didn't want to annoy him further. She hoped that the policeman wouldn't ask whether Pluver was happy to continue leasing. Thankfully, he didn't. It would only look bad for her if he found out that Pluver didn't want to lease her land any longer. Maybe that would seem like a motive for doing away with him.

"Tell me, Detective Crowley, have you located Mr. McAllister yet?" Emma wondered if she should tell him that she was there and she was the one to discover Pluver's body, but that would also implicate Maureen and she was sure that Maureen would want to keep silent on the matter. Besides, it looked as though she was enough of a suspect already. It wouldn't look good that she had been untruthful from the start.

"Yes, we have. He arrived late to the office today. He couldn't believe what had happened. He said there was a key missing, a key from his drawer."

"Is he a suspect?" Wil asked.

"At this stage, Mr. Jacobson, everyone is a suspect."

"Surely Emma isn't a suspect?" Wil asked.

Emma swallowed hard, but quickly hid her guilty expression as the detective swung around to face her. "Where were you last night between six and ten o'clock?"

"She was with me," Wil answered as quick as a flash.

Emma felt her heart pump wildly, yet she had to maintain a cool exterior.

"Is that correct, Mrs. Kurtzler?"

Emma nodded and forced a smile. She wished Wil hadn't said that; Emma was dragging too many people into this mess with her. First Maureen and now Wil. That reminded her, she had to get to Maureen fast to tell her – well, to tell all the widows – about the detective and the fact that she was most likely a suspect.

"Is that a 'yes,' Mrs. Kurtzler?" he asked again, apparently waiting for a verbal response rather than a half-hearted nod.

"Yes." Emma hated to lie, but she had done no wrong, and for the purposes of the investigation she was innocent. Surely a small fib wouldn't affect the detective's work – she wasn't guilty, after all. If the detective knew she and Maureen had found the body, it wouldn't help him in his investigation one little bit since they didn't know who'd killed Pluver.

As the detective left, Wil and Emma stood on Emma's front porch and watched the police car speed up her driveway back to the main road.

Wil slapped his hands against his thighs. "Looks like we've got another funeral to go to."

Emma nodded and thought about Pluver's

widow. She was a very disagreeable woman, and Emma was sure she'd never seen her smile – not once. Now she would have absolutely no reason to smile with her husband gone. "Wil, why did you say that you were with me?"

"I knew it wouldn't look *gut* to say you were alone here in the *haus*."

"Why? I'm not guilty of anything." In the back of Emma's mind, she wondered if perhaps Wil was giving himself an alibi by saying he was with her. *Nee, that's ridiculous – I'm getting too carried away*, she thought.

"Of course you're not, so what harm would it do for me to say that you were with me?"

Emma nodded. "I suppose so. *Denke.*" *Once again, he's come to my rescue.*

"Are you okay, Emma?"

Emma realized that she'd been staring off into the distance. She laughed a little. *"Jah*, I'm okay. Lost in my own little world."

Wil put a warm, comforting hand on her shoulder. "Do you want me to stay a while?"

Emma knew she was in dangerous territory as his touch sent tingles throughout her body. *"Nee*, I think I might go and visit one of the girls."

He then put his other hand on her shoulder and

faced her directly. "I can drive you there. You look like you're a bit weary."

She had to get away from him fast. She stepped back from his hands. *"Nee,* I'll go alone."

"You stay here; I'll hitch the buggy for you."

"Denke, Wil." Emma smiled as she watched Wil walk toward the barn. He was fine to look at; he was tall with wide shoulders and strong arms. She wondered whether the detective thought it odd that they were together so late at night, as Wil had fibbed. Being an *Englischer,* he probably thought nothing of it.

Her attention was taken again with Wil's strong frame. *It's a wonder he's never married,* she thought once more. Having Wil do something simple as hitch her buggy felt good. It was nice to have a man around.

Emma hoped that she wasn't doing the wrong thing in going straight to Maureen's *haus* to fill her in on what had just happened with the detective. Surely the policeman wouldn't follow her or anything like that. She would likely notice someone following her, anyway, because cars went much faster than the buggies. There she was, being too suspicious again. First she'd thought that Wil was using her as an alibi, and now she thought herself so interesting to the detective that he would have her followed. Maybe, with all that was going on, she was losing her mind.

She pulled up in the buggy outside Maureen's *haus* and ran to the front door. As she put her hand up to knock, Maureen opened the door.

"What happened? You look terrible," Maureen said.

Chapter Nine

And we know that all things work together for good to them that love God, to them who are the called according to his purpose.
Romans 8:28

Maureen ushered Emma inside her *haus* and they both fell into the soft couch in the middle of Maureen's living room.

"Oh, Maureen, it was terrible. I went there this morning to McAllister's office, and there was a detective there, and he started asking me questions."

Maureen interrupted, "You didn't tell him anything, did you?"

"*Nee,* hush and just listen. He said the man who was killed was Amish, and since I'm Amish and I was the first person to show up there, there must be a connection. Then he came to my *haus* and asked me a lot of questions."

"Okay, slow down. Breathe. Now, what did he ask you?"

Emma battled hard to remember what the detective had asked her. Her head was all muddled. "Well, Wil was there too, and the detective asked me how long ago my husband died and how I knew Pluver – that's really all I can think of."

Maureen patted Emma's leg. "See? Nothing to worry about."

"Oh, he did ask me where I was last night."

Maureen's eyebrows flew up and nearly met her hairline. "He did?"

"*Jah,* but Wil said that he was with me."

Maureen's eyebrows lowered into a frown. "Why would he do that?"

"I've been thinking about that. I think it's because he knew I'm alone every night and he wanted to give me an alibi."

Maureen nodded and looked thoughtful. "Maybe."

"Oh, it was awful. My heart was beating so fast the whole time he was there."

"Did Wil say anything else?"

"*Nee*, not really. He doesn't suspect a thing. He did ask me what I was doing at McAllister's office this morning, and I just said that I wanted to know more – things like what my farm would be worth. He seemed to believe that."

"That's good."

"Maureen, who do you think killed Pluver? Do you think they might try and kill me?"

"I don't know. We have to find out who killed him and why. You should go and talk to The Vulture and find out if he knew Pluver at all."

Emma made a face. "What makes you think that he'd tell me?"

Maureen shook her head a little. "I don't know, but at this stage that's all we've got. Unless …"

"Unless what?"

"Unless you go and visit Mrs. Pluver."

Emma squealed. "Me? I don't even like the woman." Emma bit her lip. That had come out before she could think. She never liked to speak ill of people. "I shouldn't have said that, but she always looks so disagreeable. I've never even seen her smile – she scares me a little."

Maureen gave a little sound from the back of her throat. "You don't have to be polite around me. I agree with you; she never looks happy."

Emma put her hand on Maureen's arm. "Why don't you come with me?"

Maureen covered her face with her hands.

"Oh, come on. Please, Maureen?"

Maureen chuckled. "All right then."

Emma pushed her head into the high back of the couch. "So, what kind of things can we find out from her? See if she knows The Vulture, I guess. That would be the first thing. We'd have to wait a few days, wouldn't we? Should we wait until after the funeral to visit her?"

"Most likely that would be best, but *nee,* we should go soon. We'll go first thing tomorrow, and maybe take Mrs. Pluver some fresh baked bread and some beef casserole."

"Good idea," Emma said.

"You bake the bread, and I'll make the casserole. I've got some nice beef already. Now, let's pick up Silvie and we'll go to Ettie and Elsa-May's *haus* so we can tell everyone what's going on."

The Amish Widow

* * *

After visiting with all the widows, Emma arrived home as the sun was going down. None of the ladies in the widows' group had any better idea than the plan she and Maureen had come up with – to go and visit Mrs. Pluver. Emma would bake the fresh bread in the morning. Tonight she was too tired to do anything.

* * *

Somehow Emma managed to get a little sleep and she had no bad dreams. She woke early, and as she waited for the bread to bake, she heard someone at her door.

"Hello?"

She knew that the deep voice belonged to Wil. Emma flung the door open. "Come in, Wil."

"Mmm, I smelled the bread and came for breakfast."

Emma laughed. "Well, it'll be ready soon. I've baked a few loaves; I'm taking some over to Mrs. Pluver's *haus* later today. I'm going there with Maureen."

"That's nice of you."

"Sit down and I'll make a pot of tea." When Wil was comfortably seated at the table, Emma asked him, "Tell me, Wil, how long was your lease to Pluver?"

"No idea. I'd have to look it up. It's a five by five lease, I know that much. We're into the second lot of five years, but I've no idea how far along it is." He leaned back in the chair. "Why do you ask?"

"Pluver told me the day before he died that he wanted out of the lease."

"Did you agree?"

"Apparently I had no choice. With Levi gone, that left Pluver with a loophole to get out of the contract." Emma shrugged her shoulders.

"I wonder what he was doing in McAllister's office," Wil said.

Emma remained silent, hoping to find out more about McAllister from Wil. When Wil offered no further information, Emma said, "Did Pluver ever tell you that he didn't want to farm your land anymore?"

"*Nee,* but he was still on the lease; I'm pretty certain it goes for quite a while. He made no mention of wanting to end the lease. I would've let him out of it if he didn't want to farm the land any longer – he was the one who wanted the papers drawn up rather than a handshake agreement so that he could be secure in his farming."

"I guess that's understandable." Emma could be silent no longer about seeing Wil with The Vulture. "Wil, I have to tell you that I saw you with The Vulture the other day."

Wil looked confused. "Really, where?"

"I saw the two of you talking and then I saw you having lunch together. You looked pretty cozy."

"I didn't see you anywhere," he replied. "Anyway, I asked him to keep away from you. Then I thought I'd make friends with him in an effort to have him keep his distance." Wil looked at her. "You do believe me, don't you? What other business would I have with the man? He did agree to stay away from you – we even shook hands on it."

Emma pursed her lips. "Did he say anything to you?"

"About what?"

"Well, what did you talk about?" Emma asked.

"He wants to buy up a lot of land. He even asked me if I wanted to sell."

Emma poured the hot water over the tea leaves in the pot. "Is he buying it for himself or is he acting as an agent for someone?"

"I'm not sure. The way he spoke, I would think

that he was buying the land for himself; I couldn't say for sure, but he is a realtor." Wil fixed his gaze intently on her. "Emma, you don't think I'm deceiving you in any way, do you?"

Emma placed the teacups on the table. "So many things have happened in such a short space of time. I guess I don't know whether I'm coming or going sometimes. I just want to feel safe again." She slumped into one of her kitchen chairs.

Wil moved to sit beside her and reached out his hand. Emma knew it was a friendly gesture, not a romantic one, so she placed her hand in his. "I'll always be here to look after you, Emma."

That's exactly what Levi used to say to me, but he isn't here now. Levi had left her alone – whether he'd wanted to or not, he'd left her alone.

Wil suddenly looked up. "Smells like the bread's ready."

"Oh, goodness me." Emma jumped up. "Just as well you said something or it might have burned."

Emma wrapped her hands in dishtowels and pulled the loaves of bread out of the oven.

Wil sniffed the air. "Mmm, they smell great, don't they?"

"They smell delicious. I'll cut you some pieces."

"I'll do it." Wil rose to his feet, took the large bread knife out of the drawer and sliced up the loaf.

As they sat and ate warm bread and butter together, Emma found it comforting to have a man in her kitchen, sitting and speaking with her.

The sound of Maureen's buggy pulling up out the front disturbed the two of them.

Wil jumped up and looked out the window. "It's Maureen. I'll be on my way, then. *Denke* for the fresh bread."

She followed Wil to the front door and said goodbye before calling out to Maureen. "Won't be a moment!"

Minutes later, Emma hurried to Maureen's buggy with the fresh baked bread under her arm.

"You two looked very cozy when you were saying goodbye. Come to think of it, he was over at your place quite early."

Emma laughed. "Stop it. He smelled the bread and came over to have a few slices. That's all. He's a friend and nothing more."

"All right. You don't need to convince me so thoroughly. Now, let's go over our plan with Mrs. Pluver."

"I do feel a bit awful going to see her since I don't really like her. I do feel sorry for her, of course – who wouldn't? It's just that under normal circumstances I wouldn't visit so soon after her husband's death."

"Relax, Emma. You think too much. We've got to do this; there's no other way around it. We've got to find some things out."

As they drove down the Pluvers' driveway, a police car was driving the other way. Emma saw Detective Crowley in the passenger's seat. The police car stopped, and the detective got out and flagged the buggy down.

"Stop, Maureen. It's the detective."

Maureen pulled the horse up quickly and Emma got out to greet Crowley.

"Ah, Mrs. Kurtzler, we meet again – that's an odd coincidence."

"Yes, I was just heading to give my condolences to Mrs. Pluver. That's what we Amish do." Emma hoped she hadn't sounded too cheeky.

"Carry on, then." The detective got back in the police car, and continued back down the driveway toward the road.

"He's intimidating. I don't like the way he looked at you," Maureen said.

"Jah, I know. He seems to be suspicious of me for some reason. I wish I hadn't gone there that morning – to The Vulture's office."

"It'll all work out in the end, I'm sure," Maureen said.

Mrs. Pluver stood at her front door and waited for them to get out of the buggy.

Maureen was the first to speak to Mrs. Pluver as they walked toward her. "We're so sorry to hear the news, Ethel."

Emma nodded in agreement and said, "We've brought you some food."

"*Denke*, come in." Ethel Pluver stepped aside to let them enter the *haus*.

Ethel made them tea and they sat down together.

"Was that a detective that we passed?" Maureen asked.

"*Jah*. You may as well know that they think that Henry was murdered."

Maureen and Emma kept silent.

"I suppose you've heard the talk already?" Ethel asked.

Both women nodded, and Emma said, "I'm afraid I found out fairly early on. I went to McAllister's office early that morning to talk to him. The police were there."

"I see." Ethel dropped her gaze away from the ladies.

"Did your husband tell you that he didn't want to lease my farm anymore?"

Ethel turned to Emma. *"Nee,* he didn't tell me anything about his dealings. When did he tell you that?"

"It was about a week ago."

Ethel Pluver looked into her tea and then set the teacup back on the table. "He was acting quite strangely, but I thought nothing of it."

Maureen cleared her throat. "Do you know Mr. McAllister?"

"Nee, I don't know him at all."

Maureen and Emma exchanged looks without Ethel Pluver seeing them. They knew they had asked enough questions. They stayed a little longer talking with her and made sure she had all that she needed. Just before they left, the bishop and his wife arrived to visit.

On the way back to Emma's home, Maureen said, "So what do you make of it all?"

"She said that Henry was acting funny – 'strange' is the word she used, I think. I wonder what that was about?"

"Mrs. Pluver doesn't know McAllister, but obviously Henry Pluver knew him, or why would he be at his office?"

Chapter Ten

Ask, and it shall be given you; seek, and ye shall find; knock, and it shall be opened unto you:
Matthew 7:7

Maureen came to get Emma to take her to Mr. Pluver's funeral. They were silent for a while as they traveled in the buggy before Maureen said, "I heard whispers that Mrs. Pluver was being unfaithful."

Emma laughed. She thought that Maureen was telling her a joke. When Maureen didn't join in with her laughter, Emma turned to see a serious look on her face. "You can't be serious."

"Well, I'm just saying what I heard."

"Unfaithful with whom? The Vulture?"

"I don't know, Emma, but you should keep an open mind about things. Where there's smoke, there's fire. Have you ever heard of that saying?"

"Jah, but Mrs. Pluver? Grouchy old Mrs. Pluver? She hardly seems the type of woman to be unfaithful. I mean, what sort of man would be interested in a cranky old lady like her?" Emma asked.

"Don't know. A cranky old man perhaps?"

Maureen and Emma giggled. Before too long, they had reached the cemetery. Maureen pulled on Emma's arm. "Look, that's The Vulture isn't it? Over there."

Emma looked to where Maureen pointed. It was indeed Mr. McAllister, and he was standing next to Bob, Mr. Pluver's son.

The widows knew they had to keep their eyes open for any strange sights at the funeral. There was one such thing that Emma noticed: the pretty young secretary from McAllister's office was there, crying. Both times Emma had seen this girl she'd been in tears. "Look up there, Maureen. That's a most odd sight."

"Jah, it is a most odd sight indeed, and I don't think it's gone unnoticed by Ethel Pluver."

Emma studied Ethel for a few moments and noticed her glancing more than once at the *Englisch* girl standing a short distance from the grave.

* * *

It was later that day that the detective came to Emma's door.

"Can I come in?"

"Certainly." Emma stepped aside for the detective to enter. "Come through to the kitchen. How can I help you, detective?"

"We have a witness who saw an Amish woman near McAllister's office at seven p.m. That's the estimated time of death."

"I see. And how can I help you with that? There's a lot of Amish women around town. Do you suspect me? Is that why you're telling me this?" Emma was sure that she and Maureen had been at McAllister's office around eight or nine.

"Mrs. Kurtzler, is there anything that you wish to tell me? If you cooperate, things will go better for you."

Emma gasped and looked at the detective in horror. "I didn't do anything, Detective Crowley, and I would never kill anyone." Emma frowned at the nerve of the man accusing her of something so horrendous.

"You were annoyed that Mr. Pluver no longer wanted to lease your land."

Emma wondered how he knew that. She didn't remember telling him anything of the sort. "It's true, he didn't want to lease the land anymore, but I wouldn't have killed the man because of it. I can't even kill a fly on a hot summer's day. Do you have any suspects – besides me, I mean?"

"I know that he was killed around seven and there was an Amish woman seen there at around that time. McAllister said there was a key missing from his office."

"What did Mr. Pluver have to do with Mr. McAllister?" Emma asked.

A wry smile crossed the detective's face. "Not Mr. McAllister. It seems that McAllister's secretary and Mr. Pluver were quite friendly, if you know what I mean."

Emma's mouth fell open. *Pluver and the pretty young girl she'd seen that morning at McAllister's office? Surely not!* "That's very hard to believe." Emma wondered which story was more likely – cranky old Mrs. Pluver having an affair with The Vulture or Henry having an affair with the young secretary. Neither story seemed plausible.

"Mrs. Kurtzler, I have to ask you this straight out – were you also having an affair with Henry Pluver?"

Emma sprang to her feet. "Detective Crowley, that is the most horrible thing that I've ever heard in my life. I most certainly was not! Please leave immediately." Emma could feel her whole body shake as she walked to open the door. The detective had to be grasping at straws – there was absolutely no basis for him to have asked her such a dreadful thing.

"I'm sorry. I didn't mean to upset you – I'm just trying to piece things together."

Emma said nothing, but held her chin up high while she showed him out the door.

When he stepped down from the porch, he turned around and said, "I might need to ask you some more questions at another time."

Emma couldn't bring herself to speak. After shutting the door, she immediately went to the window to watch him drive away. Once she was certain that he had gone, she bolted the lock on the door then walked out to her garden. She always felt peaceful in her private garden. A few minutes later, she heard Wil's voice at the front door.

"Emma!"

"I'm 'round the back, Wil."

"I saw that detective drive away." As Wil walked closer, his expression changed and he hurried toward her. "What's the matter, Emma?" He put his arm around her shoulder.

"Oh, Wil, it was horrible. That horrible detective." Emma buried her face into Wil's hard shoulder as she sobbed.

Wil lifted her away slightly and asked, "What happened?"

Emma did her best to stop her sobs and took a couple of deep breaths. "He asked me if I was having an affair with Henry Pluver."

"That's ludicrous. I don't want you talking to that detective again unless I'm here." Wil pulled her toward him and placed his muscled arms around her.

Emma let out all her bottled up emotions and sobbed some more. She was sure she was crying against him for three whole minutes before she stopped. When her sobs turned into sniffles, Wil offered her his large, white handkerchief.

She managed to smile a little. *"Denke."* She wiped her face and noticed that she had made his shirt wet. "Look what I've done to your shirt."

Wil looked down at himself. "That's the least of our worries."

"I suppose so." Emma's voice croaked. "Wil, can you take me to Elsa-May and Ettie's *haus?*"

Wil looked down at her and frowned. "Really? Why would you want to go there?"

"I just want to speak to them, and I'm sure they can bring me home later." Emma knew that she was in no state to drive a buggy.

"Of course I'll take you there."

Chapter Eleven

The name of the LORD is a strong tower:
the righteous runneth into it, and is safe.
Proverbs 18:10

As soon as Emma arrived at Elsa-May's and informed her of the latest news, Elsa-May gathered Maureen and Silvie for an emergency meeting. When they arrived, Emma explained to the widows what she'd learned – all of them except for Ettie, who was in town on an information-gathering expedition.

Emma finished by saying, "So, I can't work out

which of the stories is true, if any of them are true at all."

Elsa-May bustled over to a drawer in her sideboard and took out a notepad. "Let's see what we know so far. Pluver is dead; he may or may not have been having an affair with McAllister's secretary. Mrs. Pluver may or may not have been having an affair with McAllister."

Silvie laughed then swallowed her laughter as Elsa-May glared at her.

Maureen spoke up. "So what would the motive be to kill Pluver?"

Elsa-May looked at her pad as she wrote. "Well, Emma's just told us that the detective has a witness placing an Amish woman around the scene of the crime at approximately six, or was it seven?"

"Just around the building; I don't know if she was seen entering or leaving or anything like that," Emma added.

"Nevertheless, we're just going on the information we have at hand. If Pluver was having an affair and Mrs. Pluver found out, she would be none too happy about it."

"That's right," Silvie agreed. "We all know that mostly people are killed over money or love."

Emma noticed that the ladies all nodded. That

was something she'd never given much thought to – the main reasons for murder.

Elsa-May continued, "Now, if Mrs. Pluver was having an affair with The Vulture and Mr. Pluver found out, he would be none too happy."

"But ..." Silvie held up her hand. "What does it have to do with Pluver telling Emma he can't lease her land anymore? And what about Bob, Pluver's son? Maybe he did it so he could inherit his father's business. From what I hear, they don't get along at all."

Bob Pluver had always made Emma feel uneasy. Maybe he was capable of killing someone, even his own father. He always seemed to be skulking around and he never looked anyone directly in the eyes. In her mind, that had always been a sign that someone couldn't be trusted.

Elsa-May said, "But why was Pluver killed in McAllister's office?"

Silvie pushed out her lips. "That has to be the key to the whole thing. The reason that Pluver was in the office."

"Maybe that was his meeting place with the secretary," Maureen said.

"It's unlikely that McAllister would kill someone

in his own office. He would surely come under suspicion," Emma said.

There was silence for a while until Maureen said, "What about Wil?"

Emma turned to look at Maureen. "What about him?"

"Why was he speaking to The Vulture that time, acting all friendly and having lunch with him?"

Emma felt all eyes on her. "He said he was trying to get The Vulture to be nice to me. What? Do you think Wil might have killed Pluver?" Emma suddenly realized that Wil would also be disadvantaged by Pluver's death, unless Bob was prepared to take over all his father's leases. She hadn't even stopped to give a thought to the fact that Pluver leased Wil's land as well. Surely that meant that Wil was not a suspect.

Maureen grabbed Emma's arm. "Emma, do you still have that contract of sale that you took from Pluver's office?"

"Jah, I do, but I haven't even thought to look at it with everything that's gone on."

"Let's all go to your *haus* now and take a look at that contract."

Everyone squeezed into Maureen's buggy. Once they arrived at Emma's house, Emma took the contract from her kitchen drawer. Her eyes scanned the page until she saw the name of the potential buyer – Henry Pluver. She threw the contract onto the table. "It's Henry. He's the one who wanted to buy my land."

"So Henry does know McAllister?" Elsa-May said.

Maureen said, "Seems like Pluver was trying to buy some cheap land."

"He probably thought that he would get it cheap because of what happened with Levi," Silvie added.

"We're no closer to finding out who killed Pluver, though," Emma said.

"I'd reckon it was Mrs. Pluver," Maureen said.

"I heard Bob never got on with his father, and someone told me that last week they had a terrible row," Silvie said.

Emma turned to Silvie. "What about?"

"I don't know," Silvie replied. "I couldn't find that out."

"Maybe Bob found out that his father was having an affair and he threatened to expose him?" Maureen said.

"Who did it, Bob or the mother?" Elsa-May said, focused on her yellow pad as if that would provide the answer.

The widows all heard a buggy pull up. Elsa-May leaned back in her chair so she could see who it was. "That's Ettie. By the way she's running in the door, I'd say she's found something out."

Emma jumped up, but Ettie burst through the door before Emma could reach her.

Ettie was breathless and had to sit a while before she could speak. "I have a friend who works in the travel agency, and guess what I found out?"

"What, Ettie? What?" her *schweschder* urged her.

Ettie held up her hand. "Hang on ... Too puffed to speak." A few seconds later, she continued, "Two plane tickets, one for Henry Pluver and one for Liza Weeks." When the ladies were silent, Ettie said, "She's the secretary of McAllister."

Elsa-May scratched on her note pad and said, "So Henry had plans of running away. To give his boy security, he was trying to buy your land, Emma. It joins onto the Pluvers' land at the back."

"So if I sold, that would make him feel that he had provided for his boy at least? I wonder why he wouldn't approach me himself – why go through The Vulture?" Emma asked.

Maureen said, "He didn't want his wife to know what he was doing."

"Well, she would've found out," Silvie said.

"But not until he was well gone," Maureen replied.

Elsa-May placed the yellow pad down on the table in front of the couch and looked up at Emma. "I think we should call your detective and tell him what we know."

Emma put her hand to her chest as she recalled the detective's attitude. "He's not my detective."

"You know what I mean. I'll call him – what's his name?" Elsa-May produced her cell phone and stood up. "Don't worry, I'll call from outside."

Emma opened her mouth to say something to Elsa-May of the dangers of bringing the outside world into the *haus,* but then she stopped herself. After all, Elsa-May did say she was going to call from outside the *haus.* She made an excuse for everything she did; there was hardly any point in protesting. "His name is Detective Crowley."

"Ah, Detective Crowley. I've met him before."

Emma followed Elsa-May outside to listen to her call. It was clear that Elsa-May already had his number in her phone as she only pressed one button before she got his voice mail. Elsa-May left a message saying to come to Emma's place as soon as possible.

"Well, what happens now?" Emma said.

Elsa-May stated in a firm tone, "We wait."

Two cups of tea and three plates of cookies later, Detective Crowley knocked on Emma's door. The ladies told Crowley everything they knew, leaving out the part about Emma and Maureen being the ones to find Pluver's body in the first place.

"Looks like I'll be asking Mrs. Pluver some questions. Once again, thank you Elsa-May, and you too, Ettie." He looked at Emma, and said, "Mrs. Kurtzler, I'm sorry that I got the wrong end of the stick with you."

Emma nodded and gave the detective a forced smile, although she didn't take kindly to the man. He had as good as accused her of wrongdoing, but an apology was an apology and she had to accept it.

Detective Crowley turned to Elsa-May. "What have you got going here? A secret widows' society?"

Elsa-May remained straight-faced. "We just might have."

The ladies left soon after the detective. Emma hoped the detective would get to the bottom of things and she could feel safe once more.

Nothing seemed the same. How would she cope with no income and without Pluver's lease money? Hopefully the insurance money would come through from Levi's work, but she couldn't rely on that; Mr. Weeks had said that it was a long shot.

It was then that it occurred to Emma that Mr. Weeks had the same last name as McAllister's secretary. She was sure of it. She hitched the buggy and went to Elsa-May's *haus* as fast as she could.

She scrambled to the front door, and Elsa-May answered it with Ettie close behind her. "Elsa-May. What was the name of McAllister's secretary again?"

"Come in, Emma." Elsa-May scrambled through her notes. "Liza Weeks."

"Levi's boss' name is Devin Weeks; I wonder if they're related?"

"There's one way to find out." Ettie walked over to the same cabinet where she stored the rubber gloves and pulled out the cell phone.

Emma opened her mouth in shock. Again, Emma knew it was no use saying anything – besides, maybe the *Ordnung* would change in a few years.

"How will that tell us anything?" Emma asked.

"Emma, all young people have Facebook. We simply find her Facebook account and scan through her photos to see if we can find one of ... What was his name? Dustin?"

"*Nee,* Devin. Devin Weeks."

Ettie turned on the phone and tapped some

things. "There are a few named Liza Weeks here; which one is she?"

Emma looked at photos of three people with the same name before pointing to one. "That's her."

"Hopefully she's lax on her privacy settings," Ettie mumbled, more to herself than anyone else. "Bingo. Devin Weeks – it's her father all right, and he's got himself a Facebook account as well."

"Well thought-of, Emma," Elsa-May said.

Ettie said what they were all thinking. "Maybe Mr. Weeks found out that his daughter was going to run away with Pluver, so he killed him."

Elsa-May tapped her fingers on her chin. "Hmm, now we have another suspect."

"This is too much; I think I need to go home," Emma said.

"I'll tell the detective to meet us all here tomorrow at twelve," said Elsa-May.

"Okay." Emma agreed just to get out of the place. It was all so baffling. So many people could have killed Pluver: his son, his wife, the father of his lover – maybe even his lover herself, if they'd had an argument.

Chapter Twelve

Yea, though I walk through the valley of the shadow of death, I will fear no evil: for thou art with me; thy rod and thy staff they comfort me.
Psalm 23:4

As Emma drove her buggy past Wil's place, she saw him waving her down from the front of his house. She pulled up in front of him.

"Emma, where have you been? I've hardly seen anything of you."

"I've been spending a lot of time with Maureen and Silvie." Emma was sure that sounded more believable than spending time with the two elderly widows.

"Have dinner with me tonight?"

"I'm too tired to go anywhere. I just want an early night. I'm sorry, Wil, some other time?"

"I've already cooked chicken and vegetables. Besides, it will save you having to cook, and you can leave straight after you eat to get an early night. I'll even walk you home."

Emma knew she didn't have anything ready for dinner, but she had all that food there that the bishop's *fraa* had left her; all she had to do was heat it up. "*Denke* that would be *gut*." She decided to accept his invitation so she wouldn't have to heat up food or clean the dishes afterwards.

"Come over whenever you're ready."

Emma noticed some wood he was working with. "What have you got there?"

"I'm working on an invention. It's a new plough."

"I'll see you soon, then." Emma smiled and moved her horse on toward home. Wil was always working on some new gadget or other. She knew better than to ask too many questions; he got rather enthused when he had a project, and she wanted to get home before dark rather than listen to a long tale about the new plough.

The Amish Widow

After dinner that night, they sat on Wil's porch.

"What's the matter with you lately? You seem so worried. Is everything all right?" Wil asked her.

"Levi's just died – I'm allowed to grieve, aren't I?" Emma fiddled with the strings of her prayer *kapp*.

Wil pushed his fingers through his dark hair. "I'm sorry, of course, you're allowed to. I just meant that you seem to be worried about something else. Am I right?"

"I'm a bit worried about the farm. I'll have to find someone else to lease it, I suppose."

"Well, you'll find someone. There's a handful of men I can think of who'd most likely lease it from you. The Amish are always looking for farmland, you know that."

Emma nodded.

"Anything else?"

Emma looked up across the darkness of the fields in front of her. "I'm worried about who murdered Henry Pluver."

"Emma, you can't spend the rest of your days worrying about things."

Emma looked into Wil's eyes. He never seemed bothered by much at all. If he had any advice for her, she would like to hear it. "How can I spend the rest of my days, Wil?"

"Spend them with me, as my *fraa*."

Emma laughed a little and put her fingertips to her mouth to stifle her giggles.

"I'm serious, Emma. I want to look after you and protect you from harm."

Emma didn't know if he loved her or just wanted to look after her. She wouldn't marry again unless it was for love. *"Denke* for your offer, Wil."

What followed between the two of them was an awkward silence. Emma considered it best to go home. Wil walked her the five minutes to her house.

As Emma lay in bed that night, she considered Wil's offer. What was to become of her, all alone? Sure, Maureen and Silvie were young and alone, but were they happy? What better man would there be for her in the whole community than Wil? Maybe she should seriously consider his offer, even if he were not in love with her. She could see herself falling for him, but did he feel the same? If he were in love with her, surely he would have said as much.

Emma closed her eyes. She felt she'd been on a very fast horse for a very long time, and she wanted to get off and just have a quiet, normal life without worrying about who had killed Pluver and why.

When Emma woke up the next morning, she decided to pay Mr. Weeks a visit at his work before she met with the widows at Elsa-May and Ettie's place.

She knew that he worked out of a van at one of his construction sites. The van had been converted into a high-tech office.

She had the taxi drive her straight to the site, which was deserted except for Mr. Weeks' car parked near his office. She walked up to the van and knocked on the door.

Mr. Weeks pushed the door open. "Mrs. Kurtzler, come inside."

"Hello, Mr. Weeks. I hope you don't mind me calling in on you unexpectedly."

Mr. Weeks shuffled the papers that were on his desk into a drawer. "Not at all. What can I do for you? Have you come to find out about the insurance claim?"

"Well, not really. I came to find out about your daughter."

Mr. Weeks sat down in his chair. He motioned for Emma to sit in the other chair. "What about my daughter?"

"Is Liza Weeks your daughter?"

"Yes, she is."

"Did you know about the rumors regarding Liza and Mr. Pluver?"

"Come for a walk with me, Mrs. Kurtzler." At her question, Mr. Weeks' face had contorted into someone whom she didn't recognize. She was scared to go for a walk with him, but she needed some more information.

Mr. Weeks pointed to the door, and Emma turned and stepped through with Mr. Weeks close behind her.

"Your husband was a valued employee."

"Yes, he was a hard worker."

Mr. Weeks pointed to the building that was not yet complete. "This is not the building your husband fell from."

Emma nodded as she looked up at the unfinished building. She hadn't wanted to know any details.

"Let me show you the view as we talk." Emma followed Mr. Weeks into an elevator at the side of the building.

"I'm a little afraid of heights." She looked at the small elevator. "And closed-in spaces."

"It's a lovely view from the top. I'd like to show it to you. It's quite safe; the other side has a viewing platform where we take potential buyers."

Emma hesitated at the door.

Mr. Weeks added, "It's passed all safety regulations."

Emma stepped into the elevator. *Maybe there were private papers that he didn't want me to see in his office, and he might feel better walking and talking at the same time,* she thought.

As they rode in the elevator, Mr. Weeks said, "I know that my daughter was set to run away with that old man."

"You knew?" The elevator stopped and Mr. Weeks held the door for Emma to step through.

Once she was out of the elevator, she turned and waited for Mr. Weeks to answer.

He nodded. "I wouldn't let that happen. I knew she was slipping away at night to see someone. I had her followed, and she was going to your property, to the barn at the end of your farm."

Emma recalled the rarely used barn at the end of her property as well as one close to her home.

"That's why I thought it was your husband she was going to run away with – because it was your farm she was meeting the man on. I didn't know that Pluver had a lease on your property. I found out soon after."

A chill ran down Emma's spine. "No, Levi would never do anything like that, never."

"I found that out too late, Mrs. Kurtzler. I'm very, very sorry. I didn't mean it to happen like this."

Was he saying what she thought he was saying? If he thought Levi was having an affair with his daughter, then maybe he killed Levi and maybe he also killed Henry Pluver. Emma didn't know what to do. She asked meekly, "What are you sorry for?"

"I didn't mean to kill him."

Emma's hand instinctively flew to her heart. "You killed Levi?"

Mr. Weeks' face was grim as he slowly said, "I had to kill him. I had to protect my daughter. When I visited you at the farm, I knew it wasn't your husband I was after. I lodged that insurance claim for you."

Emma covered her mouth; she felt as though she would be sick. It was much worse that Levi was killed at the hands of a madman rather than in an accident. Emma knew she'd made a big mistake by going to see him alone, but she wouldn't let this man do the same thing to her as he'd done to Levi and to Pluver. She looked out of the corner of her eye for an escape route. "You killed Pluver, as well?"

"I had to stop him ruining my daughter's life." Mr. Weeks took a step toward Emma, and she stayed very still. "You don't have children, do you Emma?"

Emma shook her head.

"When you have children you'll do anything to protect them. Anything."

Emma glanced behind her and saw that there was a sheer drop, five floors down. "Well, your secret's safe with me, Mr. Weeks. I won't tell anyone."

Mr. Weeks laughed. "I'm afraid I can't trust you with the information I've just given you." He walked toward her.

Emma pleaded, "No, don't kill me. They'll know that you did it."

"No, they won't." Mr. Weeks laughed again, and his eyes flashed with the black evil of the devil himself. "You were so distraught over your husband's death that you killed yourself."

Emma closed her eyes so she wouldn't have to look at him. "No one will ever believe that."

"They will if that's how I say that it happened." Mr. Weeks was three paces from her and he closed the gap between them quickly. His face turned white and his hands shook as he stretched them out towards her.

There was nowhere for her to go and nothing she could use to defend herself. Emma sank to the floor and closed her eyes. She prayed – she didn't want to die, not here, not like this.

Chapter Thirteen

But without faith it is impossible to please him: for he that cometh to God must believe that he is, and that he is a rewarder of them that diligently seek him.

Hebrews 11:6

"Weeks, put your arms in the air!" A voice boomed through a microphone.

Emma opened one eye and saw Mr. Weeks had his hands in the air. She closed her eyes and continued to pray.

The voice boomed again. "Step away from the lady. Make one false move and we'll shoot."

Mr. Weeks took a step away from her. Sirens of police cars sounded; there would have been at least two, maybe three.

"It's all over, Weeks!" The voice boomed once more.

Emma opened one eye just slightly to see Mr. Weeks lowering his arms and taking a step toward her.

"Keep your arms up or we'll shoot."

Weeks raised his arms.

Emma glanced over the side of the building to see two uniformed policemen getting into the elevator. Mr. Weeks remained silent with his arms straight above his head.

Emma must have blacked out for a moment, because when she next opened her eyes she saw Mr. Weeks being handcuffed by two police officers.

Another officer ran toward her. "Are you hurt, miss?"

Emma shook her head.

"Stay still," the officer ordered. "We've got an ambulance coming."

Emma watched Mr. Weeks being led into the elevator.

She closed her eyes and thanked *Gott* that He listened to her prayers. "I'm fine. I don't need an ambulance. I'm fine." Emma went to stand up, but her legs were like jelly. "Maybe I'll stay here for a few moments."

"I'll stay with you," the officer said.

Emma sat on the floor, and all she could think of was Wil. She was certain that she wouldn't feel safe until Levi's strong arms were around her, but they never would be again.

Detective Crowley appeared out of the elevator. He walked over to Emma while shaking his head at her. "What did you think you were doing? You nearly got yourself killed."

She was still slumped on the ground. "I didn't know he was a murderer – I was just going to ask him a few questions." Emma heard her voice and it didn't sound like her own; it was much more high-pitched than normal.

"Well, you're very lucky. When you didn't turn up at Elsa-May's place, she thought you might have done something silly. Ettie and Elsa-May figured out what happened. They went to find you when you didn't show. They then called me and told me what their suspicions were."

"I'm so pleased they did."

"They do have their ways about them. Let's get you out of here. Are you okay to move?"

"I'm okay." Emma got to her feet and then rode down in the elevator with Detective Crowley. She had nearly gotten killed – murdered. Nothing seemed real to her anymore.

The paramedics arrived on the scene quickly afterward. She was given the all-clear from the medical staff, but was told to rest. Crowley had a policewoman take Emma home.

* * *

When Emma opened her front door, she was never more pleased to be there.

She sat on her couch, wrapped herself in a blanket and waited for Wil. She knew it wouldn't take him long to get there to find out why a police car had just been there.

"Emma!" Wil burst through the door without knocking.

Threads, who had been lounging on the rug near the door, bolted out of the room at the sudden noise, his claws skittering across the floorboards as he disappeared into the kitchen.

Wil sat next to her and asked all the questions

that Emma knew that he would. She answered them all, leaving out the part about nearly being murdered. He didn't need to worry about her anymore than he already did.

Emma glanced toward the kitchen, wondering if the cat would return. Threads never ran from her—but maybe he sensed the whirlwind of emotions in the room, just as she was trying to make sense of them herself.

"Emma, you can never do anything silly like that again." He moved closer and put his arm around her. "You should never have gone there." He pulled her toward himself, and she rested her head on his shoulder. "Do you want me to get you anything? Some tea or some soup?"

"*Nee,* I couldn't have one thing." Emma sighed. "But perhaps you could drive me to Elsa-May and Ettie's *haus* tomorrow."

"Of course."

* * *

It was eleven in the morning when Emma arrived at Elsa-May and Ettie's place; Ettie phoned Silvie and Maureen, and it didn't take them long to show up.

The group was finally assembled, and each

woman hugged Emma tightly and made a fuss over her. They had all heard what had happened from the detective.

Ettie made Emma a strong cup of tea with three heaped teaspoons of sugar, saying she needed the sugar to help her get over the shock. Elsa-May insisted that she stay wrapped in the warmth of a blanket. Emma tried to explain that she was fine and not in shock; after all, it had happened a whole day ago.

Emma was glad to be alive and finally safe. She didn't even mind sitting on the hard wooden chairs in Elsa-May and Ettie's living room.

"So, Mr. Weeks killed Mr. Pluver because his daughter was going to run away with him? He originally thought that his daughter was having an affair with Levi and killed him too?" Silvie asked.

Emma was too shaken to speak. Maybe she *was* still in a little bit of shock.

Elsa-May spoke instead. "That's right. And I guess Pluver wanted to buy the land so he could give it to his boy, Bob – maybe to appease his guilt from leaving, who knows."

Emma's thoughts turned to Wil – she hadn't given him all the information. She had told him that Mr. Weeks had killed Levi, but she hadn't told him that she was nearly murdered as well. How could she have ever thought that Wil could have anything to do with deceiving her over her land? She smiled a little as she remembered his proposal.

Yes, it was most likely too soon after Levi's departure and tongues would wag, but Emma decided she could overlook that, just as she had overlooked Elsa-May and Ettie's cell phone. The first time she'd married for love. Would the second time be for companionship, and just to feel safe?

Maureen interrupted her thoughts, "Does Wil know about all this?"

"Some. I told him the main parts."

"Ettie called Wil and he's coming to take you home," Maureen said.

Emma frowned. "Wil's only just brought me here."

Maureen smiled widely. "He answered his phone in the barn when Ettie called him. He said he'd just arrived home."

"Why is everyone fussing? I'm fine, and I've only just gotten here. Anyway, surely someone else could have taken me home." She looked at the widows in turn, and each one smiled at her. "You're all up to something," Emma said.

"*Nee* we aren't," Elsa-May insisted.

Half an hour later, Ettie said, "I hear a buggy."

Elsa-May walked over and lifted Emma to her feet.

"There's nothing wrong with me, Elsa-May. I'm just a little shaken. Well, I was shaken yesterday, but today I'm fine."

Elsa-May opened the door to Wil.

"Emma, are you all right?"

Emma could feel her cheeks flush. She wanted to run into his strong arms, but she couldn't, not with all the ladies around. All she could do was nod in answer to his question.

"Well, I'll get you home." Wil looked up at the ladies and smiled. "*Denke* for calling me. Good day, ladies."

It was clear to Emma that the ladies were stifling giggles as they said goodbye to her and Wil.

As Wil led her to the buggy, Emma said, "You must have only just arrived home before having to turn around and come get me."

Wil glanced over at her. "I'm not about to say no to anything Elsa-May asks me to do. She scares me."

Emma laughed, but had to agree. Elsa-May was a very forthright woman.

As soon as Wil's buggy was out of the sight of the house, he pulled over to the side of the road. "Emma, what did you think that you were doing? I nearly lost you." He touched her cheek softly with the back of his hand. "Ettie told me everything. She guessed that you wouldn't have told me all that happened."

Emma closed her eyes and savored his touch. "I don't know what I was doing. I didn't know that the man was a murderer."

"You're safe now, so that's all that matters. I'm going to get you home and look after you properly."

Emma giggled softly and looked into Wil's eyes. A flicker of guilt touched her heart—because she still loved Levi. She always would. But grief didn't mean she wanted to be alone forever. The silence in the house, the emptiness—it had worn her down. Wil had been part of her past, yes, but in that moment, she saw something else in him. A steady hand. A kind heart. Maybe... just maybe, Gott was gently opening the door to her future.

To every thing there is a season, and a time to every purpose under the heaven: A time to be born, and a time to die; a time to plant, and a time to pluck up that which is planted;
Ecclesiastes 3:1-2

Samantha Price

* * *

Thank you for reading The Amish Widow. See what the widows get up to next in their next adventure. Book 2: Hidden

A mysterious stranger. A suspicious death. And a secret the widows can't ignore...

When an elderly Amish man is found dead under unusual circumstances, the women of the Amish Secret Widows' Society are once again on the case. But just as the investigation heats up, one of the widows is swept off her feet by a charming outsider claiming he wants to join their peaceful community.

Book 2: Hidden

About Samantha Price

Samantha Price is a USA Today bestselling and Kindle All Stars author of Amish romance books and cozy mysteries. She was raised Brethren and has a deep affinity for the Amish way of life, which she has explored extensively through over a decade of research. When she's not writing, Samantha enjoys cooking and spending time in nature, where she finds peace and inspiration for her stories.

www.SamanthaPriceAuthor.com

All Samantha Price's series

For a downloadable/printable Series Reading Order of all Samantha Price's books, scan below, or head to: SamanthaPriceAuthor.com

Amish Maids Trilogy

Amish Love Blooms

Amish Misfits

All Samantha Price's series

The Amish Bonnet Sisters

Amish Women of Pleasant Valley

Ettie Smith Amish Mysteries

Amish Secret Widows' Society

Expectant Amish Widows

Seven Amish Bachelors

Amish Foster Girls

Amish Brides

Amish Romance Secrets

Amish Christmas Books

Amish Wedding Season

Shunned by the Amish

Amish Recipe Books

www.ingramcontent.com/pod-product-compliance
Lightning Source LLC
LaVergne TN
LVHW021456220625
814403LV00009B/312